A DOG'S BREAKFAST

Phil Teller

D1488081

Acknowledgements

To Albert who made me promise to write this book.

To Linda who made me keep the promise.

To Chelsea who provided the material.

To Mary who made me believe I could do it.

And to Krista who gave me the wisdom and insight I needed.

Table of Contents

THE REDHEAD

That girl you hang around with is crazy you know, ...
Whacked—I don't know where you find these people.

She fits the profile to a T.
Redhead.
Probably from the planet Argon or something, ...

I've never met anyone who would optimize your refrigerator just for something to do.
She's brilliant, but she's crazy.

We had such a blast that night we took her out into the desert—
What a night!

She reminds me of a racehorse in the starting gate just before the bell.

Being around her is like having a narrator to your life—
A moment-to-moment running commentary on what's happening in the world around you.

Let me give you some advice.
You need to listen to what she says.
She's the key to your success, you know,
To getting what you've always wanted.
But you have to listen to what she tells you, ...

Someday you'll finish that book, and you'll be rich.
Then you can retire and go live by the lake like you've
always dreamed.

You need to stop working so much and just be a writer.
She'll help you if you let her.

Redheads are like that.
If I can give you one piece of advice, it's this:
Listen to that redhead—do what she says.

She'll make you famous someday.

THE MORNING AFTER

"Farm-fresh, organic, lightly speckled brown eggs," he read, "from free-roaming hens with access to the outdoors, shade, fresh air, and direct sunlight. Provided with clean water, given lots of exercise, and fed wholesome organic food that's grown without the use of pesticides or herbicides."

The penmanship was exquisite. The wide architectural style, the block-print lettering with perfect kerning, the open As and elliptical Os, every comma in place, every period just right.

"Hormone and antibiotic free, ultra-pasteurized, 2% reduced fat, vitamin A and D milk from a local dairy where the cows are automatically milked, warm washed daily, and free to graze on gently sloping pastures of fresh green grass in The Great Pacific Northwest."

He thought he recognized the trademark quality of the Sharpie ultra fine point pen she had used. He glanced at the thick glass coffee table a few inches from his knees, flawlessly placed for ideal feng shui in front of the glove-leather suede couch upon which he sat, and there it was. Of course, she had chosen the one with the soft-grip barrel and the delicately hinged chrome clip, the effortless glide of the ink delivery, so consistent throughout the writing process, regardless of paper or hand pressure.

"Fresh Seattle bread," she had written, "with only the very finest organic ingredients, having the delicious taste of stone-ground wheat, steel-cut oats, and crunchy hazelnuts; zero grams of trans fat, not a hint of high-fructose corn syrup, and slow baked for ultimate flavor and texture."

He heard her coming down the hall from the bathroom as he continued to read: "Fresh Washington State apple juice, low-moisture, part-skim, rBST-free cheese, robust, organic, fair-trade coffee, succulent, vine-ripened, heirloom tomatoes. One locally grown, new-harvest, Walla Walla sweet onion."

She was barefoot and wore only white silk panties and an oversized, organic bamboo tank top. With her long red hair flowing over her shoulders, she was every man's dream of the perfect woman to wake up to.

"What's this?" he asked, holding the sheet of ultra-white, heavyweight vellum paper in his hand.

She smiled, showing him the most perfectly corrected teeth he had ever seen. He noticed the seductive movement of her bare breasts beneath the baby-skin soft fabric as she moved closer to see what he was holding. She smelled like a wicker basket filled with fresh tangerines.

"Oh, that?" she chuckled. "That's just my shopping list silly. I'm going to cook you a delicious breakfast."

He glanced at her radiantly glowing face and morning-after hair and asked, "Are you a . . . writer?" She laughed casually and said, "Yes, I am. I got my MFA in writing from Western Washington University."

"You're from Bellingham?"

"No," she said, collecting a few intimate things from the arm of the couch, "I'm actually from Bellevue, and now I live here. I lived in the dorms while I was in school, but that was ten years ago. I loved Bellingham. I took as many classes as I could on the Fairhaven campus."

'Fairhaven. Hippie college,' he thought to himself, trying his best to appear nonchalant as a chill ran up his spine. His hand trembled ever so slightly as he held the list between his fingers. He felt a little dizzy as he began to understand the reality of the truth he was facing; he felt it roar over him like a speeding freight train. A simple classified ad for a rowing machine had brought them together only eighteen hours before . . . and now . . . fate would tear them apart.

He had assumed she was probably an English major—so well versed, so articulate—but he would never have guessed she had gone all the way to a master of fine arts degree. His face flushed as he thought about the potential consequences of a future with a writer; she, clicking away alone on a shiny new Mac-book Pro, he, listening to National Public Radio instead of watching The Big Game on Sunday. What would his friends think?

What would his *family* think? For a split second he imagined the horror of . . . an outdoor wedding.

"How long have you been writing?" he asked, frantically trying to reignite the conversation, internally grasping for some positive outcome.

"Since I was about six," she joked cheerily over her shoulder, as she ambled gracefully toward the kitchen to start a pot of coffee. "I learned to write when I was in the first grade."

He laughed inappropriately loud and tried desperately not to imagine a room full of pretty little girls all in a row, holding fat pencils and scrawling neat letters on big paper studded with little bits of wood fiber. It was so sick and wrong. He tried thinking about No Child Left Behind, but it was no use. He knew what he had to do. He'd been here before; he knew there was no future in it. He had accidentally dated a librarian once, and he still carried the scars she'd left on his heart.

He also knew that writing was not a choice for her. She was born to it, like the emerald-green color of her eyes.

She selected a pair of delicate porcelain cups from the cupboard and set them on the expansive marble island with a musical clink.

He calmly placed the list on the glass table where he had found it and rose to his feet. "I'm sorry, but I'm afraid I can't do this," he said. "I have to go."

She stopped spooning coffee into her expensive French coffee press and gazed at him, confused, as he gathered his coat from the back of a chair at the kitchen table.

He paused to savor the look of her one last time. "I had the time of my life," he said. "Really." Then he headed for the door, leaving her staring and stunned in her spacious, open-floor condominium overlooking Elliot Bay above Pike Place Market.

He hesitated another moment and rested his hand on the brushed nickel handle of the large maple door then said, "Last night was wonderful, you have no idea" he paused as he struggled to find the words, . . . but I just can't do this." He said.

"Do what?" she pleaded.

"This . . . all of this," he replied, gesturing with a brief sweep of his arm. "You're a writer, and this isn't going to work for me. He gazed at her for a long moment then said, "Thank you so very much, for everything, but I have to go now."

He reached into his coat pocket to find the keys to his Camaro. "Maybe we can e-mail or something," he said, letting himself out, making sure to turn the lock on the inside of doorknob as he left.

He walked down the wide concrete hall and stepped into the stainless-steel elevator, pushed the button marked P that would take him to the subterranean parking lot, then slumped against the wall opposite the doors and thought for a moment about a life with a writer. The staring eyes of gawking strangers, the frightened looks from passing children. She would never find a decent job. She probably cooked while listening to . . . *opera.* The thought of it made him queasy.

As the elevator doors closed, he gazed at the ceiling in resignation and thought to himself, *Oh my god, that was a close call. That was really, very close.*

THE WISE COUNSELOR

Many years ago, at a time when I was reluctantly in counseling prior to my impending divorce from my first wife, my counselor, a brilliant woman with godlike insight, asked me why I thought my wife wanted to leave me.

"She says she just doesn't love me anymore," I told her with a lump in my throat and tears trying to escape my eyes.

My counselor looked at me for a long moment, as though she was waiting for me to recover from the information I had just given her, or maybe she was waiting for me to prepare myself for the information she was about to give me, or maybe she was just composing a response.

Her reply came more easily than I would have expected, like a line from the script of a movie on the thirty-seventh take. Her face softened, she leaned forward a little and spoke more sympathetically than she had before as she asked me quietly, "Why would you want to be with someone who doesn't love you?"

I broke like a dropped wine glass. I cried hard—for the recognition of the truth, for the understanding of my losses, and for the joy in my heart for finally being released from that relationship.

She watched me for several minutes as I wept into my cupped hands, then she wrote a quick note in her book and without saying a word, she left the room.

I have carried her words in my heart for all the years since then. I will never forget them. Never forget the meaning. Never forget the importance, and never forget to ask myself that vital question she asked me, when I am not completely secure in any kind of relationship with anyone. "Why would you want to be with someone who doesn't love you?"

I DO NOT WRITE

I do not write.
Each day I rise with the sun, and each day I toil.
And I do not write.

I hear the music in my head and sing the songs I have
known so well for so long, and yet I do not write.

I eat my morning fruit and drink my daily tea.
I feed the livestock and feel their soft and grateful
humming.
I see their thankful eyes, but I do not write.

I smell the new spring lilac and magnolia, but I do not put
pen to paper.

I do not touch the coveted and elusive white plastic of my desktop friend, my lover, my life, and allow my fingers to tap out the staccato rhythm of the contents of my head.

How I suffer in this unbroken darkness of silence, for I am not writing.
I am not telling you of my loves and likenesses.

My heart beats slowly in my chest. How it longs to rush through the tall grass, feel the wind on its face, and smell the earth as the sky weeps through the singing trees.

I long to write.
My heart knows the finish line is near.
Time becomes more precious with each passing hour, and still, I do not write.

THE FLIGHT TO RENO

On a recent flight from Seattle to San Francisco—a stopover on my way to Reno—an attractive and intelligent woman with the graying temples of wisdom and the crow's feet of experience, took the seat next to mine. She was wearing an expensive scarf wrapped around a neck brace, and she almost immediately engaged me in interesting conversation.

Having flown this route on many occasions, I have been most often accompanied by strangers who would otherwise be on a Greyhound bus or didn't speak English, or simply had nothing more to say than, "How you doin'?" Some have been even less forthcoming than this, on much longer flights.

Not the case this time. This woman was very different. She was effervescent, well educated, and witty. We laughed and shared our life stories, our differences and similarities, and it seemed we were barely airborne when we were already descending into California.

I asked what she did in real life, and she told me that she spent most of her free time skydiving. As she spoke she unconsciously adjusted her neck brace, implying that her injury was indeed somehow leaping related.

Thinking I was being clever, I asked the same-old, worn-out question she'd no doubt heard a hundred times before: "Why would someone jump out of a perfectly good aircraft?"

She hesitated for the briefest moment and smiled at me with perfect white teeth and said, "Because the door is open."

She was my kind of woman, and she gave me exactly the answer I would have expected. It was hard for me not to just get off the plane with her in San Francisco, if only to see what happened next. Of all the airline trips I have taken over the years, this is the only one I can absolutely remember in every delicious detail.

YOU

I opened the door to my heart just a crack,
And the genie that lives in there leapt out to embrace you.

He dazzled me with fireworks, great magic tricks, and
wishes galore.

Now free from the bonds of his tiny domain,
I find I am powerless in my attempts to stuff him back
inside.

How addicted he is to the opium of your love.
How imprisoned in the capture of your eyes.
The rapture of your embrace.

THE CAREGIVER

She stepped out of her rubber slippers, shrugged her shoulders backward, and the silk, flower-print robe she wore fluttered off her slender, naked body. She draped it over a nearby deck chair and eased herself into the clear, light-blue, 102-degree water.

From the opposite side of the hot tub, he glanced up from his book, projected an outward appearance of disinterest, and then went back to reading.

"Hello," she said. "I'm Elaine."

"Hello, Elaine, I'm Jack." He said, momentarily looking up from his book as she settled herself across from him, then pretended to return his attention to the page.

She stretched herself out across the large, white, fiberglass hot tub.

"Are you a member or a *visiting* nudist?" he asked as he folded a dog-ear into the yellow pages of a well read Tom Robbins novel.

"You could say I'm a member I suppose," she replied as she closed her eyes and slid a little deeper into the warm, clear water.

Her head and breasts protruded above the surface as she continued. "I have that cabin up there," she said, turning her head in the general direction of a small section of cabin roof that was barely visible through the old-growth forest on a hill in the near distance above them.

"Oh," he said, "You're *that* Elaine. I've heard about you. Aren't you one of the original members or something?"

He set his book on the decking that surrounded the tub as she slowly moved to more of a sitting position and ran her hands over her thinning silver hair.

"I suppose I am *that* Elaine," she said wistfully. "I've been a member here for a little over forty years, but I haven't been around for a while. I live in Spokane now, and it's been hard for me to get away."

"Forty years?" he said. "You can't possibly have been a member that long. You don't look a day over thirty-five."

She smiled. "You're very gracious, but I am well over thirty-five, even though I still feel like I'm twenty-one. Except that somewhere along the line, some old woman traded her body for mine."

She pulled at the age-wrinkled skin on her face then slid back into her reclining position on the other side of the tub from him.

"So what do you do in real life?" he asked, a trick that he'd learned, to get people to talk about themselves, years before in a sales seminar.

"This *is* my real life." She said. "I lay around in the hot tub or drink tea with my bird. The rest of the time I work as a caregiver for dying people."

"You have a bird that drinks tea?" he asked quite seriously.

"No," she smiled, almost laughing, "I drink the tea. My girlie bird eats my muffin and nuzzles my ear."

"What do *you* do in real life?" she asked, mocking him ever so slightly in a friendly and inviting way.

"Professional liar," he replied without hesitation.

"Really?" She sat upright.

"Yep."

"Does that pay well?"

"For some folks it does, I suppose," he said, "but I haven't been in the game long enough to retire yet."

"Really?" She tilted her head to one side, pondering him. "So how can I believe a thing you say to me?"

"I'm not working right now."

She raised her eyebrows and grinned at him. "What exactly is it that you do as a professional liar?"

"I write fiction," he said. "The rest of the time I'm a professional hot-tubber."

"Really?"

"Yep, I was on the 1999 Pro Hot-Tubber's tour. I'm in training for my big comeback."

"Good luck with that," she laughed as she slid back into her comfortable reclining position.

Elaine was ten years his senior at seventy years of age, but her skin was still tight against her body, her breasts still well defined, and there was a beautiful face behind the crow's feet and smile lines that gracefully defined her age. She stretched herself out and allowed her body to slowly float to the surface. He could see that her pubic hair was still as brown as it had been forty years earlier, the mound of it between her legs still every bit as attractive as any he had ever seen. At first he averted his gaze until he was sure she had closed her eyes, only then allowing himself to stare with reckless abandon at the forbidden invitation before him.

When he had enjoyed the sight of a sinewy, wet, naked woman for nearly long enough he slid back into a reclining position, leaning his head against the edge of the tub, and stared up through the clear, corrugated-fiberglass roofing above them to the steel-gray drizzling sky.

"I used to be a model," she said quietly. I had a big career in the fashion industry. Now I take care of people who are dying. I thought modeling was tough. That's nothing compared to this."

He didn't respond, hoping she would continue. She looked wistfully at the treetops and watched a gray jay flit from a nearby branch to the back of a deck chair and then disappear into the surrounding forest.

"How'd you get started doing that?" he asked, profiling her as he had been trained to do in a college negotiations class a lifetime ago.

"A few years ago," she began slowly and directly, "a friend of mine, a girl I had known from high school, called me from out of nowhere and asked if I would come and visit her. We weren't really close after we graduated—I hadn't heard from her in years—but I had known her all my life. She was the first friend who ever asked me to spend the night at her house, so I went over to see her.

"She'd been living not ten miles from me for all those years, and I thought she had dropped off the planet. When I saw her she didn't even look like the same person, she was so frail and thin. She had always been so beautiful. She was very popular in school, and all the boys were after her, and now, here she was, wasting away, living alone in a tiny house. She told me she was dying of leukemia."

Elaine's voice broke, and she took a deep breath in an attempt to recover. She turned her head to one side, and a single tear wet her cheek. She wiped it away quickly.

Beneath the clear, hot water he gently reached for her ankle and took it in his hands. She pulled away slightly at first, thinking he had touched her accidentally but as he began to massage the ball of her foot, she closed her eyes and relaxed.

"I never left," she continued. "I stayed there for almost four weeks. I went home and packed a little bag and stayed with her right up until the end. I slept on her couch and took care of her from then on."

After a few minutes of silence, she went on with her story. "One night I tried to get her to eat some soup, but she was so weak that she couldn't get a spoonful down. She asked me if I would just hold her for a while, so I got into bed with her and wrapped my arms around her and smoothed her hair and held her close to me."

Elaine looked straight up at the clear cover above the hot tub as she spoke, and a tear rolled from the corner of each eye and down the sides of her face.

"She finally went to sleep while I was holding her . . . and then she was gone."

She allowed him to gently run his fingers between her toes and along the arch of her foot. She relaxed completely and closed her eyes as her arms floated at her sides. She didn't say anything for a while, but her face told him she was enjoying the simple pleasure of his touch. A quarter of an hour passed before either of them spoke again.

"She had been my best friend for a couple of years when we were young, but we shared so much more in those last few weeks. More than some people do in a lifetime. I felt like I knew her better than I knew my own husband. I had fallen in love with her in that short time. Not like romantic love, but real love, and when she was finally gone, I knew that she had given me the most precious gift anyone can give. She had given me herself. She gave me the experience of sharing her last moments on earth, and that was something. That was *really* something."

She sobbed just once and covered her face with her hands. "I'm sorry," she said quietly after a moment or two.

"So am I," he whispered.

He slid across the hot tub to lie next to her and closed his eyes. He slipped his hand into hers, and she accepted it without saying anything. They lay drifting side by side in the light mist of the warm water as it met the cold autumn air. The gray, drizzly afternoon eased its way toward evening like a young lover on his first date at a drive-in movie.

"That's why I came here," she said softly. "I've been taking care of dying people ever since, but I have to get away from that once in a while and spend a couple of weeks in the cabin now and then, so I can get a little of my own life back."

They lay together in silence, naked in the steaming water as the drizzle turned to rain on the fiberglass roof above them.

"I love it here," she whispered.

"So do I," he said.

She turned her head to look at him, "Are you busy right now?"

"I'm busy relaxing here in the hot tub with you," he replied.

"Are you hungry?"

"I suppose I could be hungry," he said.

"Would you like to walk up to my cabin with me and have some supper?"

"I'd love to have supper with you. What are we having?" he asked.

"I don't know," she said, moving to a sitting position, preparing herself to step out of the tub. "Why don't we just go up there and see if Raoul left anything in the microwave."

"Who's Raoul?" he asked as they stepped out.

"Oh, he's a character I wrote in a story a long time ago," she said, "He's my imaginary Latin lover, housekeeper, and cabana boy. Do you like Top Ramen?"

"I love Top Ramen," he said. "You didn't tell me that you're a writer, too."

"I have nine books in print," she said as she stepped into her rubber slippers. "I didn't want to scare you off before we had a chance to get to know each other."

MY FATHER'S OLD CAT

I don't know why he put no fish in my saucer today.
I marched on his old chest as he slept.
But he stayed sleeping.

I sang him a morning song.
But he did not wake.
I rubbed against the leg of our old chair
and gave him several backward glances.
He did not seem to notice.

I looked out our window and saw that jerky, little gray
guy that I played with yesterday.
He ran up our tree.

I saw the blue one looking at me with her darting black
eyes.
That one fluttered away.
I wished I could play with her, too.

He slept so quietly this morning.
And then he was gone.

With the many strange footsteps.
He went with the large black shoes.
The unusual scents.
He left with the shiny metal clicks and snaps.
With the long, slow zip he left, and he gave me no fish.
He has been gone a long time now.
There is nothing I can do but wait for him to come home.
To fluff my tail.
To rub my chin.
To give me some fish and cool milk.

If I sing for him maybe he will come home.
He must know I am a little hungry.
He can't be gone much longer.
He didn't kiss me or say goodbye.

He always says goodbye.

THE MIND WRITER

Built on a pier right over the water with a sweeping view of Puget Sound and the south shore of Vashon Island in the distance, the place was a moderately expensive dinner restaurant once the sun went down. But just past noon on a cold and rainy Wednesday, a single section of tables on the waterfront end of the building was only half filled with elderly locals and businessmen in for the daily specials on the lunch menu.

She sat alone at the far end of the bar and wondered for a moment how fifty-five years had raced by so quickly. She carefully sipped her White Russian, trying to make it last as long as possible while she waited for her friend April to arrive.

When she could, she made small talk with the metro-looking, thirty-something bartender, but he was too busy pouring drinks for the brunette Barbie-doll waitresses to engage in an actual conversation.

The room was filled with the sound of silverware and clinking glasses and the muffled rumble of several separate conversations occasionally broken by outbursts of laughter.

She glanced at the time in the upper-right corner of the overhead flat-screen television, where sports announcers silently handed off the play-by-play of a silent basketball game, there above the bar. Apparently April was going to be late—as usual.

She'd called April's cell phone a couple of times— once to say she was almost at the restaurant and again as she waited for her drink—but she got no answer. She assumed April was walking her dogs and had—as usual— lost track of the time. She was seriously considering gulping her drink and going back to her life. But just then a guy walked in.

He was very good-looking, could have been a movie star's brother. He had an air of casual confidence about him.

"What up, dawg?" he said to the bartender as he pulled himself onto a barstool one seat away from her and appeared not to notice she was there.

He clearly knew the bartender, so she assumed he was a regular. Probably someone who lived nearby. . . .

"What are you drinking?" the bartender asked as he spun a small, square napkin across the bar toward him.

"Bring me a Mexican beer—heterosexual!" he replied.

"Heterosexual?"

"Yeah . . . no fruit!"

She got the joke and turned away so he wouldn't see her laughing to herself.

The bartender grinned wide and said, "Ah, okay, coming right up." He pulled a longneck bottle of yellow beer from the cooler behind the bar.

"Glass?" he asked.

"Bottle." the guy replied.

Was that a Texas *accent?* She thought to herself. When she knew he wasn't looking she checked his starched, white dress shirt, his ironed blue jeans rolled at the cuff, and the worn, dark-brown hiking boots he'd hooked at the heel to the lower rung of his barstool. She could tell a lot by the shoes a man wore, and these shoes spoke to her.

The bartender snapped the cap off the frosty wet bottle and set it on the bar napkin. The guy opened his wallet and laid a five-dollar bill on the bar.

"Order!" sang a waitress from the service bar at the other end of the room. The bartender made a swooping motion with his arm and quick-stepped in her direction.

The guy took a short drink from the bottle, set it back on the napkin, and spun himself on his chair to look directly at her. "Drinking alone in the middle of the day?" he asked, as though he had known her all of his life.

"No," she said politely, "waiting for a friend."

"You from around here or somewhere else?" He asked.

"My friend lives just up the hill," she said, pointing in the general direction of the window.

She focused her attention on her drink, using the little plastic straw to stir the ice that floated in her beige concoction, trying her best to appear disinterested. He continued to look directly at her until his staring made her uncomfortable.

"How about you?" she finally said. "You from around here or somewhere else?" she asked, mocking him ever so playfully.

He took a swig from his beer. She guessed he was in his mid-forties—crow's feet but no gray hair. She watched his hand as he placed the bottle back on the bar: short nails, not bitten, skin still slightly tan well after Labor Day, not pasty white—definitely not a computer geek or video gamer—and no disgusting, telltale layer of dirt under those nails, so probably not hard-core unemployable. And *someone* was clearly doing his laundry.

"I live up at Park Ridge," he said, jerking a thumb over his shoulder.

A condo, she thought to herself. *Not a renter. That could be a good sign . . . if he's single.*

"You live there alone?" she asked.

"I've got a roommate," he said.

An ambiguous answer, she thought. *A roommate means he could be into sports and living with some slob guy, or he's shacking up with a girlfriend.*

"I'm staying with my mom," he continued. "She's getting old, so I'm helping her out for a while."

She swiveled her barstool so she was facing him. "How old's your mom?"

"Just turned sixty," he said.

Great, she thought, *either I have one foot in the grave, or I'm talking to a high school kid who's skipping school.*

"What kind of work do you do?" he squinted one eye at her as he took a short pull off his beer.

He was showing interest in *her* instead of just going on and on about himself. This was unusual. And did she feel the tiniest little throb in her nether regions? God, it had been so long, and he was so good-looking, and he hadn't said a word about sports.

"I'm an author," she said. "And I teach writing."

"You're a teacher." he said, apparently not hearing the author part, which was obviously far more impressive to her than to him. He picked up his beer and took another drink, tipping his head back a little while keeping his eyes trained on her. She felt herself blush at the attention.

"I am more of an instructor," she said. "I teach aspiring writers how to write to the formulas that the publishers are looking for."

"So do you teach at a community college or something?" he asked, making all the wrong assumptions as far as she could tell.

"Actually I travel all over the country conducting three to four-day seminars," she said, trying to impress him. "I stand on a stage and read a textbook to a couple hundred people who could just as well read the book on their own, but they feel the need to be led like sheep, down a shining path of mediocrity and literary failure, so they pay me an obscene amount of money to do the work for them."

She was trying to be funny and sarcastic, but her ironic wit was actually way over his head. She felt a warm glow in her belly. Was it the liquor she was feeling or some pheromone he was producing at a level she couldn't consciously detect?

"I'm a writer, too," he said.

"Really?"

Her interest reignited. She prayed he wouldn't tell her he was a science-fiction writer or maybe a comic book guy—the kind who wrote in drab, linear, paragraph-long sentences lacking anything that resembled an actual metaphor or nuanced thought. *Everybody's a writer,* she thought to herself. She profiled him a little further to see if he was actually trained or not.

"What do you write?" she asked, half pretending to be genuinely interested. At that moment she didn't care if he was a landscaper, she was imagining him taking her—with reckless abandon—right there on the bar.

"I'm a mind writer," he said casually.

Now she was interested. She hadn't heard of mind writing before—probably some New Age discipline with a guru and expensive weekend retreats. She smiled, showing him the thirty-two pearly whites that had cost her as much as a new car.

"What genre do you write?" she inquired casually.

"I write mostly heinous crime stuff."

"Really?" she prompted him.

"Sometimes I do a little soft porn, sometimes I mix the two together. I mostly do slasher crimes though. Axe murder stuff. I try to come up with inventive new ways of killing people. You know, the old boy-meets-girl story, then he ties her up and strangles her to death over several hours with her cell phone charger cord, then he stuffs her body in the dog food grinder at the rendering plant where he works. Right now I'm working on a story about a guy who flies to Reno, commits a random evisceration on an airport TSA agent in the men's room. He flushes the man's spleen down the toilet then hops the next flight home without leaving any other clues for the cops."

There were only a few soft-porn-slasher-crime-axe-murder writers she had ever met in person—most of them really ugly and overweight with far too much dandruff. He had clearly developed a style, specific to a captive audience. She tried to recall if she had ever seen his picture on the back cover of a paperback, those gorgeous chocolate-brown eyes . . .

"So, tell me more about mind writing," she said. "Where did you study?"

What she really wanted to know was if he was just an English major from a community college or if he actually knew something about writing. It was a trick question. If he mentioned Robert McKee or so much as hinted at a well-developed focal character or arch-plot method, she was ready to leap into his arms.

He took another drink of his beer, put the bottle on the bar, and hesitated a moment before he answered. She could see him formulating his response for a desired effect. She hungrily waited for him to enrapture her.

"I never really studied the formal art of writing," he said. "I just like to do mind writing."

"*What?*" she almost said, but instead she smiled and looked him directly in the eye as an invitation to continue.

"So . . . what exactly is mind writing?" She asked, she was expecting to be very impressed.

"Mind writing is where I write a story in my mind. I just think it up and then go over and over it in my head until I have the whole story. Sometimes I can do it in a couple of days, sometimes it takes weeks or months to get it just right."

She struggled to get a handle on what he was telling her.

"Are you published?" she probed.

"I don't write my stories down," he said, "I don't want to waste all that time and paper, so I just write in my mind."

"You write soft-porn-slash-crime in your head?"

"Pretty much." He said nonchalantly. He momentarily turned his attention to the game on the overhead TV and pumped a fist into the air. "Yes!" he exclaimed.

She was horrified. Her scalp itched. She was engaged in a conversation with a guy who lived in an apartment with his mother and made up horrific axe murder stories and thought about them for months at a time. And to think that not two minutes before, she was thinking this guy was somehow attractive.

Her cell phone rang. She visibly jumped as her fight-or-flight response kicked in. She snatched up her phone in an involuntary response and whipped it open, saying "Hello!" a little too brightly to be appropriate to the moment.

It was her friend April.

"Well, there you are!" She said with a lilt in her voice. She faked a sad smile. "Oh, honey, I am so sorry to hear that," she interrupted, in the middle of April telling her why she was going to be a few minutes longer.

"No, that's fine," she said, "I can absolutely come up there."

April was completely confused.

"No, really, I can leave right now."

She looked at him, knowing he was eavesdropping on her conversation, and shrugged her shoulders apologetically.

On the other end of the phone line, April asked her what the hell she was talking about.

"I'll see you in a few minutes," she said. "I'm leaving right now." She clicked the *End* button before April could say another word.

"I'm sorry," she said, "that was my friend. He's having car trouble, and I have to go and rescue him . . . *again.*" She laughed inappropriately.

She dug a ten-dollar bill out of her purse and laid it on the bar. She looked for the bartender, but he was engaging a blonde hottie in conversation at the waitress station a mile away at the other end of the bar, so she snapped her purse shut and slid into her beige overcoat as she stepped down off her barstool.

"It was really nice to meet you," she said.

"Nice to meet you, too," he said, extending his hand.

She pretended not to notice the gesture and headed for the door.

"Maybe I'll see you again sometime," he said as she walked past him.

"Maybe if I live to be a hundred," she thought to herself.

"Maybe!" she called to him over her shoulder.

Her heart was racing, and that was not sexual arousal, she had to pee, but there was no way she was going to spend another minute in the same building . . . in the same state . . . with that *guy.*

Out the front door, she casually looked to see if he had followed her and was relieved to see he hadn't. She dashed across the street to the parking lot and pushed the

Unlock button on her key fob. She jerked open the door, quickly got into her black Lexus, locked the doors, and started the engine. Pulling the gearshift into DRIVE she said out loud, "April, I am going to fucking wrap your cell phone cord around your neck and strangle you!"

She drove a mile up the hill toward April's house and thought to herself, *"No, April, I am going to introduce you to that guy . . . and let him do the job for me!"*

She pushed the gas pedal a little harder as she rounded the final uphill curve and snarled, "Mind writer—fuck *that*!"

CLOSE YOUR EYES

Close your eyes.
Breathe deep.
Clear your mind.
Relax your body.
Leave the work of the day somewhere in a neat bundle for a future time.

Imagine the universe, ever expanding, ever growing, ever speeding away from its own creation. Immense galaxies of indefinable size, over unimaginable time, slowly moving outward, ever away, ever more distant, toward a future of only clouds and gasses.

Try for a moment to comprehend that in the entire universe, on all of the planets, through all of the history of it all . . .The probability that you and I would somehow find each other and share this moment together.

THE CRITIQUE

Please, please, please, hide that horrible vehicle. It makes our street a laughing stock, and we believe it is negatively affecting our property values. At a minimum, it cannot be on the street for more than twenty-four hours without moving. If we have to stare at it every day, at least put it in your driveway. You are inflicting your own sense of garishness on all of us that do not want to participate.
Thanks.
—Unsigned and mailed to my home address with no return address.

Note: There are about a dozen homes in our neighborhood, and we know who our friends are. You are not hiding your identity by not having the honor to sign your typed note.
Typed?
With a typewriter? Whoa, that is so cool. No, really!
Ok, for that, I will concede one point for creativity.
Might I suggest, though, that to improve your grade point in the future, you try your hand at cutting words out

of a magazine and pasting them to a piece of colored construction paper?

Also, the line should read: . . . *all of us* **who** *do not want to participate.*

After reading your work, I find I am compelled to wonder if parking a rented Porsche or Mercedes in front of my home would somehow *positively* affect the value of your property.

I do like the use of the word *garishness,* though.

Nice vocabulary.

For that I would give the piece a grade of C-.

It is below average in requisite content and appeal.

And it lacks adherence to good storytelling guidelines.

Ed.~

THE CONVERTIBLE

Please, don't go yet.
Please.
Stay here with me just a while longer.

Laugh with me again and recall the time we rode rented
bicycles on cobbled streets so very far away.
Remember the fun we had playing together when we were
young, you and I.
When we fixed that old car.

Stay.

Tell me again about when you were a boy and you were
in the war.
About how it was always winter then, and you were
always waiting.
Waiting to move to the front, waiting for supplies to come
from the rear, waiting to go home, waiting until you could
sleep once more in your own warm bed.
I love hearing those old stories over and over again.
You said you spent a lifetime waiting then, in the war.

Don't go quite yet.
Please wait just a little longer.
There is still so much I have to tell you.

I got an old car.
It's convertible.

We could go for a drive together in the country and smell
the smells of the huge trees that overhang narrow,
winding roads.
We could feel the sun on our faces, the smooth
excitement of the fast, powerful car.
There is still time.
We could go together now.

Please don't leave quite yet.
Stay, and we can talk wistfully about owning that boat .
together, you and I.
Of sailing away just as you have always dreamed.
You and I could sail away to someplace warm,
with clear blue water and white-sand beaches.
We could smell the women baking in the sun.
Please stay, and I promise one day we will sail away.

I need you to stay just a little longer.
I am not ready to be alone.
I have grown so fond of having someone to call each day.

I still need to know that you are proud of me.
That someone still loves me after all this time.
I need you to know that I love you, that I have always
loved you, and that I will always love you.
I have not said this to you as many times as I need to yet.

Please stay with me.
Please!
I am not ready for you to go!

Please.
Dad.
Dad?

A PAINTED HOUSE

"Who are you in love with?" he asked quietly as they walked side by side, more gliding than walking, no destination in mind, just moving together in the same direction as they spoke softly of their lives.

She smiled and glanced at the sky, then answered, "Well, my family, of course, and my cat. She is my ever-faithful companion. And my daughter, I love my daughter more than my next breath, but she has her own life now.

"I have some good friends," she continued, "but love?" She hesitated to think for a moment. "I would have to say that the only true love I have in my life right now is my daughter. That will never change," she said, smiling.

They walked in silence for a few paces, then she turned to him and said. "Tell me about when you were a kid. Where did you grow up?"

"Hawaii," he said.

"Hawaii? That must have been amazing! What was that like?"

"We were poor. I had four sisters, and my mother was a cocktail waitress."

"It still must have been nice just to be able to live there. What do you remember most?"

"Moving into a painted house."

"What do you mean painted?"

"Well, it was a big deal when we were finally able to move into a house that had paint on it. The house we lived in when I was eleven wasn't painted. It was more of a shack than an actual house. It was only a little bigger than the living room of the house I live in now. We didn't have glass in the windows, just rusty screens."

They walked without speaking again.

"So what do you believe in?" he asked.

"I'm a Hindu," she said.

"That doesn't answer the question," he replied.

They both smiled.

"You don't look much like a Hindu."

"What do you think Hindus are supposed to look like?" she asked.

He stopped and stood before her and examined the details of her face.

"I suppose Hindus could look like anyone," he said.

Smiling, she asked him, "And what do you know about Hinduism?"

"I know that Hindus believe that all life is connected. That it is all the same, and that we do not own the earth but borrow it from our grandchildren, and that we should return it to them better than we found it."

"I suppose all those things are true."

They stood facing each other, looking into each other's eyes.

"What do you believe?" she asked him, almost whispering.

His mouth felt as dry as a bed sheet hanging on a line in summer. There was a lump in his throat, and as he began to speak he thought for a moment his eyes would fill with tears. "I believe," he began, . . . "that more than anything in the world right now, I would very much like to kiss you."

She stopped, turned to face him, and slipped her hands into his. She smiled and whispered softly, "I would like that very much."

FEATHER MOSS

I don't want to go home.
Not quite yet.

The trees still seek my friendship,
and the quiet of this place is still too enrapturing.
I toil away at the soft earth; smoothing, blending, stroking
the land with blistered hands.
Breathing in the silence, knowing that,
as the orange rays of sunlight land lightly on the toes of
my dirty feet, another world impatiently awaits my
presence.

The necessary tasks and agendas call to me.
The demands.
The requirements.
The imprisoning list of assignments, that do all so
desperately request my immediate attention.

Yet, still unrequited, the emerald green feather moss
invites me to lie down.
It promises to stroke my sweating brow,

To tend my battered body and softly kiss my cheek.
It beckons me, "Stay."

How I long to listen to the feather moss and obey its
sweet request.
My other world, I suppose, can wait a while longer.

CLASSROOM RULES

No smoking.
No drinking.
No spitting.
No gum chewing.
No nose picking.
No attempting to fart the "Star Spangled Banner."
No abusive swearing.
No pistol waving.
No knife throwing.
No screaming the F word.
No screaming the N word.
No name calling.
No bullying.
No coercion.
No extortion.
No blasphemy.
No attempted bribery.
No explicit sexual innuendoes or gestures.

These are the classroom rules that have been set down as behaviors that will not be tolerated. Under any circumstance.

I promise that I will do my very best to *try* to follow them while teaching my classes.

THIS MOMENT

This is my favorite moment.
When at last you come to me in the night, in the soft blue
moonlight.
To wrap me in cool sheets,
To kiss me deep, and loving.

I will choose this moment.
This one.

The one where you play your sweet sleep music for me.
Then finally touch me with your tenderness.
For this, this . . . is my favorite moment.

I will choose this moment as you gently slip into my
arms.
When I am so hungry to hold you at last.

Whispering that you love me, bringing tears of joy to my
fleeting soul. This is the moment I do love most of all.

I will choose this moment, when I can breathe unconsciously, and feel nothing but the warm softness of your skin against my body, your breath on my face. Your fingers tracing the outline of my heart.

It is said that when a soul departs this existence,
it takes with it a single moment of the life it has known
. . . to carry into the next.

This one moment.
The moment that a *soul* chooses to carry with it on its journey, it is said, is what we have come to know as heaven.

I choose this one.

OH, JACK

"No," I said, "let's check into one of those little old-fashioned motels. They're cheaper, and I like the quaint little rooms; they're so much more romantic."

She gazed longingly out of the car window at the bright-blue Holiday Inn Express sign and said, "That's fine. It says 'no vacancy' anyway."

"Those chain places are all full of people who have kids."

"Oh, yeah," she agreed. "All those kids. . . ."

We drove further down the road toward the very outskirts of the little seaside tourist town on a peninsula, in the middle of the Washington State coastline. It was late—well past nine o'clock—and the few places we had checked were already full.

She casually pointed to a sign that read 'Westerly Motel' and said, "That one looks nice."

It was a '50s-style motel right out of the movie *Psycho*. I thought it looked perfect. Pulling into the u-shaped driveway, I parked in front of a handcrafted wood sign that read OFFICE. An extremely bright-red neon sign in the front window screamed VACANCY and shone so brilliantly in the rainy darkness that I had to shade my eyes with my hand as I stepped out of the car.

In the blinding red light I could barely make out the words RING THE BELL FOR SERVICE etched in upper case letters into a small, plastic plaque next to the door. I pushed the white plastic button, while she stood politely waiting with her back to the building, gazing out into the cold, drizzly night at a single passing car that hissed by on the oceanfront road.

We waited a minute or two before we heard the muffled sound of footsteps. A light came on inside the office and an attractive white-haired woman appeared at the door. With a welcoming smile and an insistent wave of her hand she said, "Come in, come in!"

We shuffled into the warm little office that had clearly once been a family's living room. A hyperactive pug dog with bulging eyes rushed to greet us with licks and jumps and danced in circles at our feet.

The walls of the office were covered with plain, rustic wood paneling, the only furniture a small wood filing cabinet, a simple wood desk, and a single wooden chair. Down a short hallway we could see the tidy living spaces where her husband watched a television program.

Family pictures and religious icons lined the walls. Crystal and porcelain knickknacks were perfectly placed along the windowsills and rested inside several antique curio cabinets.

The room would have been a cozy place of business were it not filled with the excited actions of the pug, who now frantically sniffed at the cuffs of my jeans as he continued with his energetic panting and circling, perhaps hoping we had come specifically to visit him. He looked up at me and grinned then turned to offer me his backside so as to display his oversized asshole. I could tell by his actions that he very much wanted me to get to know him better, but I purposefully ignored his invitation.

Clearly getting nowhere with me, he lost interest and quickly went to have a look at the sights between my companion's thighs.

The dog's attention now elsewhere, I smiled at the motel owner and asked, "Do you have a room?"

The woman flashed an apologetic grin. "I have one with a double bed for forty-five dollars."

I whipped a freshly casino-won, one hundred dollar bill from my pocket and waved it in the air. "Sounds perfect. Do you take cash?"

"Oh, we just love cash!" The woman smiled and pointed to a small form clipped to an ivory-colored plastic clipboard lying on the desk. "Just sign in right over there."

"Do we have to use our real names?" I asked.

Genuinely entertained, she grinned widely. "You can sign in as anybody you like!"

"We'll use our real names," I replied as I seated myself at the desk, "but you'll have to promise not to tell the prosecutor."

The woman laughed and made a cross over her heart with her forefinger. "I promise!"

I handed her the hundred and turned to sign the registration form. She went to get change from a silverware drawer in the kitchen.

Standing near the door as I wrote, my companion bent down to pay attention to the dog to distract it long enough to allow me to fill in the blanks with a steady hand.

She rubbed at his ribs and laughed as he went into a frenzy of tickle-scratching with a hind leg. He was frenetic by the time the motel owner returned.

"Your total with tax came to forty-nine dollars and seven-two cents." She carefully counted the change out into my hand then took a room key from the pocket of her apron. The key had a homemade fob with a large 12 etched onto it. As I reached to accept the key, she squinted at me playfully and asked, "You aren't an international terrorist are you?"

Before I could respond, my companion replied in her most engaging southern accent, "He is *absolutely* an international terrorist."

"Well, then," the woman said, "this means *you* get the key." The motel owner laughed as she reached over my shoulder to hand the key to my obviously more trustworthy companion.

We said goodnight to the woman and her pug, but the dog's continued antics indicated he would much rather go with us than stay with her. The woman managed to coax him to her and picked him up as I opened the door to leave. The lure of the outside world caused him to squirm and struggle in her arms, but the door closed, thwarting his wild attempt to run headlong into a manic exploration of night smells and the world beyond.

Outside, we got back into our car and drove to the other side of the parking lot, pulling into a space directly outside room number twelve.

Parked in the space in front of room eleven was an absurdly tall, four-wheel drive pickup truck that had all the big truck accessories one could imagine: giant chrome wheels, huge, fat tires, over-sized exhaust pipes, a tube steel chrome brush guard, and matching step rails. The rear bumper was nearly as high as the roof of our car. There was a gun rack in the back window and a pair of leather testicles hanging from the hitch.

I handed my companion the key. Without noticing the truck, she stepped out of our little car, unlocked the room door, and went inside with an armload of coats and handbags while I opened the hatch and retrieved our overnight luggage. I stumbled through the door as she was turning on the lights and turning up the heat.

She gazed briefly through the bedroom door then turned to me and said, "This is very cute!"

I could see that look in her eyes, and I knew what she was thinking. She opened the door across the narrow hallway and said, "What a cute bathroom! I have to pee."

She went inside and closed the door. I dropped our bags onto the sculptured carpet and plopped down on a flowered wing chair in the small living room to rest from the long drive.

Almost immediately I began to hear a light thumping sound coming from the opposite wall—an obviously identifiable and steadily rhythmic, thump, squeakita, thump, squeakita, thump.

I heard the toilet flush from behind the bathroom door, and a moment later she walked unwittingly into the living room.

Thumpida! Thumpida! Thumpida! The noise increased in intensity and rhythm as she became aware of what was going on next door. She grinned at me with a mischievous twinkle in her eye. I put a finger to my lips and mimed an exaggerated sexual movement with my hips as she turned back to stare in amazement at the wall.

Thumpida! Thumpida! Thumpida! The noise grew quite loud now, and there came the sound of a woman's voice, "Oh . . . oh . . . oh. . . ." keeping perfect time with the steady thumping of what was clearly the headboard in room number eleven banging against the wall.

She smiled at me and put her hand to her mouth, quashing a laugh. We said nothing and listened in entertained amazement as the ruckus continued next door.

THUMPIDA! THUMPIDA! THUMPIDA!

"OH, OH, OH, UH, HUH!"

THUM, THUMP, THUMP! The woman in room eleven was now screaming in ecstasy. The banging on the wall came harder and faster as she screamed, "OH, OH, OH, OOOOOH, JACK! OH, JACK! OH, JACK! OH, JACK, OH!"

With exaggerated facial expressions and body movements, we began to pantomime what we imagined to be the scene on the other side of the wall as the thumping and moaning continued and then slowed, finally fading to complete silence until once again there was quiet in our little rented space.

"What the fuck was that?" I whispered.

Smiling mischievously she quietly replied, "Must have been a happy ending."

I silently mouthed, "Oh, my God," as we tried our best to muffle our laughter and stumbled arm in arm to the bedroom.

We laughed and giggled as we peeled off our clothes and climbed into bed. I rolled onto my side and reached to turn off the light on the little antique nightstand then wrapped myself around her and buried my face in her neck.

She held me tightly, and we kissed hard and passionately as we hugged each other. Our legs entwined, our hands gently rubbing each other's bodies, embracing.

The sweet flower scent of her hair falling across my face, I kissed her deeply. She invited me into her, and I gently eased myself there and whispered, "I love you—I have always loved you—I will always love you. . . ."

I felt her catch her breath. Holding me closer, she began to cry softly "I love you, I love you, I love you. . ."

I slowly withdrew and eased my way into her again then did not move. She rhythmically rocked her hips so very gently and whispered into my ear, "I love you, I love you more than I have ever loved anyone," her voice breaking as her tears wetted my cheek.

She pressed her hips hard into mine.

"Oh . . . my God," I groaned softly.

"Oh, *Jack* . . ." she whispered.

ANGEL

Driving south on U.S. Route 395 in north central Oregon on a stormy winter morning in early January, my only child was on her way home to Nevada after visiting her extended family here in Washington for Christmas.

She had stayed with my wife and I, and visited for a few days in Seattle then driven to Spokane to be with her mother and Eastern Washington family until after the holidays.

Beautifully happy and twenty-eight years old, she was miles south of Pendleton on a bare and dry roadway, traveling at the posted fifty five mile per hour speed limit.

It was snowing hard that day, so even though it was far too cold for the snow to more than blow across the highway, she had, as instructed by her husband and her common sense, engaged the electronic four-wheel drive feature of her SUV and was listening to the radio, almost three-hundred miles into her seven-hundred-fifty mile trip. Without warning, on a long, sweeping curve of the two-lane road through a pine forest, her truck began to slide sideways on a large patch of ice that appeared out of nowhere.

Knowing just what to do, she took her foot off the gas and gently counter steered as I'd taught her, but the six-year-old Ford did not respond and crossed the centerline. She slid perpendicular to the direction she had been traveling and braced herself as she skidded off the highway into a snow bank. A microsecond later her car slammed head on into a steep earth embankment—more roadside cliff than gentle slope—just a few feet away.

From what she can remember, her Explorer ricocheted off the frozen embankment so hard it went airborne, stood momentarily on its nose, pivoted, and then landed on its wheels to face the direction from which she had been traveling.

From the injuries she sustained, the hospital staff surmised the car slowed dramatically as it left the roadway and traveled through the mound of snow left behind by passing snowplows. Her doctor said that hitting the frozen snow bank probably caused her to lurch forward in her seatbelt. Her face must have been inches from the steering wheel when the SUV struck the embankment and the airbags deployed explosively, fracturing the bones around her eyes and nose, blinding her by the impact.

They said that she probably flew upward and out of her seat as the car crashed into a handstand position, sending her into the interior light and the rear-view mirror, smashing the light to pieces and jamming the mirror into the windshield with her forehead.

The car then landed again on its wheels, and she fell back into the driver's seat, seriously injured and momentarily unconscious.

She remembers waking up to the smell of gunpowder from the air bag going off and not being able to find the release for her seatbelt or the door latch because she couldn't see.

Temporarily blinded by the impact of the air bag and bleeding heavily from her facial injuries, she kicked her way out through the window of the driver's door that was now sprung shut by the twisted truck body.

Wearing only a tank top and jeans in the sub-freezing temperatures, she stumbled her way to the edge of the roadway and screamed for help, frantically waving her arms at the sound of passing cars.

Kneeling on the frozen ground, bleeding into the white snow, she waited and waved at the sound of each passing car as it went by.

It was hours later in rush-hour traffic in Seattle, 250 miles away, just after dark in the pouring rain, when she told me the story by cell phone from her hospital bed.

I was emotionally wrecked by the call, and haunted by the thought that of my bleeding daughter crying for help next to a wrecked car in a snowstorm. Why would no one stop to help her? Why would someone just drive by giving her no more regard than a dead animal alongside the road?

For the remainder of the drive home after that call, I couldn't help wondering: Is this what we have become? Is this is how we treat each other now?

Do we now use our post-911 fears as an excuse for indecisiveness and inaction? Do we simply refuse to see or acknowledge the existence of another person in desperate and immediate need?

Do we no longer know what to do when we see a fellow human being in trouble? How awful does an accident have to be before someone has the courage to stop to help when a person is clearly injured?

Is dialing 911 the only response we have left? No matter the circumstance? Even on a mountain highway . . . in a blizzard . . . in the middle of nowhere?

Have we lost the ability to see that this isn't downtown Yourtown U.S.A., and that the cops won't be there in the next three minutes if we call?

Is this what they have done to us as Americans? Have we become so fearful, so impartial, so callous that we just slow down, look, and keep going?

I couldn't help wondering if that many people could be *that* afraid or unaware of a young woman bleeding and begging for help alongside a desolate road in a blizzard that they wouldn't stop to so much as ask if she was okay.

I found myself feeling a little sorry for those people. The ones who just drove by as my daughter waved and screamed for help. I know they saw her; it was the middle of the day. And I know they had to make a conscious decision to do nothing as the stinging snow blew hard onto my child's bare and bleeding arms.

I know they saw her broken and blood-covered face, and I know that the memory of her leaning against a snow bank, waving for help along that snowy road will be with them forever.

I am thankful I did not have to witness that level of heartlessness firsthand. I am thankful I am not one of those who just drove on by, for I would not want to carry that kind of karma through the rest of this lifetime or into the next, and I hope that this is *not* the America we have become.

My child pleaded for help for over twenty grueling minutes until one exceptionally compassionate woman, on the way to visit her own children, skidded to a stop and rushed to help her.

An off-duty paramedic—a fellow nurse—came to my daughter's aid and put my child, freezing in the seven-degree temperature, into her own car and drove to a hospital three-quarters of an hour away.

She stayed in the emergency room with my only child and waited for hours while the medical team sewed my daughter's bruised and broken body back together.

I thank God there was an angel on this planet that day who, after calling a towing company while on the way to the hospital, knew to take my girl, once released to her care, to where her car had been towed and to help her collect her most intimate and personal belongings—her purse, her phone, and her warm winter coat—before driving her to another city, one closer to an airport where she might somehow get back home.

Central Oregon was in the middle of a blizzard that day, and all the mountain passes between my child and me, were closed, along with all the airports. Neither her mother in Spokane nor I in Seattle, could get to her until the weather subsided.

I thank God for the one individual on this planet with enough compassion, and empathy, to drive eighty-four miles out of her way to a motel where my girl could rest and recover.

And then this angel stayed with my badly injured and blinded daughter for an entire night until my child's mother, distraught beyond consolation, was finally able to arrive in the early hours of the following morning to take her only baby home to Reno on a plane.

Although I am not a religious man, I thank God that there is an angel out there in this world, still caring enough to know the simple things to do when she sees a fellow human being in need.

This woman did the unthinkable: She stopped to help a complete stranger who could not help herself. She did the honorable thing: She took time out of her own life to lend a hand to someone in desperate need and refused to leave until my daughter was safe and sound in the loving arms of crying family.

And though I have never met this woman—this angel on earth—I now humbly bow to her with my deepest and most heartfelt gratitude and offer this, my solemn pledge in her honor:

From this day forward I vow to lead a better life.

In her honor I will be a better person.

I will seek out and find ways to help others as she helped someone who means so much to me.

This woman is a true example of the meaning of compassion, caring, and responsibility, and I will hold her up as an example of how I shall aspire to live my life from this day forward.

Each grateful tear of thanks that falls from my eyes this day reminds me of the debt of gratitude that I will forever owe her.

And although there is no way I can ever repay her for what she has done for our family, in her presence I would fall to my knees in humblest respect and kiss the very ground she walks upon; this angel on earth.

"Thank you, Myla. You will live in our hearts forever."

RIDING OFF INTO THE SUNSET

"Pigeons are funny guys," she says. "They are really smart. Most people hate pigeons, but I just love to watch them when I'm waiting at the bus stop. The males always know when a female is around. They puff up their chests and stand up real tall and strut by, looking sideways. They say 'Coo!' and the female always looks away as if to say, 'Yeah, right, whatever.' Just like in real life."

She laughs. I love it when she laughs.

"I love to watch the crows, too," she says. "They are far more intelligent than most people credit them." She takes a sip of her iced green tea and glances wistfully out the large window behind me. She is watching an old, hunched Chinese man shuffle in the direction of the train station.

"When I'm at the Renton Transit Center there are always a group of pigeons looking at me sideways." She mimics a pigeon and smiles impishly. "They want to know if I have food. They're all like, 'You got anything?' They check me out a few times to make sure. 'You got anything? Anything?' Then when I don't give them anything they strut off like, 'I didn't want anything from you anyway.' "

She looks directly at me, her ocean-blue eyes smiling, hands folded under her chin. On her finger I see the gold glint of the ring I gave her so many years ago, and I can feel my heart wallow in my chest. She is the single most beautiful woman I know. We are waiting for the train to come and take us across the country.

"We are going to be riding off into the sunset," she says, looking west with a smile. The thought of riding off into the sunset with her makes my heart skip a beat. Everyone knows that when it is true love, they always ride off into the sunset.

THE TIDE

The tide goes out, and as the water recedes into the coming sunset,
I see the vision of my life.

And it is there that I hear the sound of your voice,
beyond the murmur of the rippling waves,
flowing endlessly onto this cold, gray sand.

The tide goes out so slowly,
and I hear your laughter in the call of the far-off seabird,
like the heartstring sound of a singing child.

So slowly it goes as the rain washes away the traces of its leaving.

And as I watch it go, I remember your love,
fading into the twilight that rainy autumn day.

I watch the tide go out,
and I remember longing to hold you one more time.

To feel your heart against mine, like the rhythm of the
ever-changing sea.

I remember your breath, like this salty rainwater breeze
on my face,
as I stand on the cool beach and watch the receding tide,
like the bits of memory that are lost day by day,
as time grows between us.

I stand here and watch the leaving sea,
and it reminds me of the love we had given each other—
the kind words we had once said in the quiet moments
and wish there had been just a little more.
More time, more loving, another look into your eyes.

As the tide goes out, I wander alone on this beach and
wonder . . .
Would it matter if I had God,
or if I loved Jesus?
Would I somehow find redemption, some forgiveness in
my loss
or in our last goodbye?

I held your hand and wept as your face turned the color of
this cold, gray sand,
and I begged you not to leave me.
It was like begging this tide to stay.

You smiled and said, "Farewell." And went with the tide
that day.

"Do your best," you said as you turned to go, waving,
and wearing that smile,
the one that will forever be etched into the fabric of my
soul.

"Do your best. And remember who loves you," you said.
"Remember who loves you. . . ."
And then you left.
With the tide.

On that cold and raining autumn day.

THE HELICOPTER INCIDENT

Carol knocked on the door of her sister Pam's tiny, second-floor apartment. She heard footsteps in the hall, and a moment later the door latch clicked.

"Ohhhhhhhh!" Pam sobbed as she opened the door and saw Carol.

"Oh, honey! What *happened*?" Carol asked as Pam fell into her arms. Carol patted her gently as a mother would comfort a crying child.

"He's *gone*!" Pam cried. "And I don't know what I'm going to do!"

"Who's gone?" Carol asked quietly.

Pam was inconsolable. "Mic . . . *chael*. . . ." she sobbed.

"Now, now, tell me what happened," Carol said, trying to comfort her younger sister.

"Michael was *killed*! In a horrible accident!"

"Oh, sweetie, that's *awful*! I'm *so sorry*! Tell me everything. How did this happen?"

"He was on call . . . as usual . . . when . . . when there was a huge storm. . . ." Pam sobbed with her face buried in her hands.

"Oh, darling, tell me all about it," Carol said as she steered her sister inside and closed the door so the neighbors wouldn't see.

". . . And there was a flash flood . . . "

Carol held her gasping sister in her arms and guided her down the hall to the living room.

". . . And they went out in the helicopter, and they rescued a family that was clinging to a tree, and there was a ten-year-old girl . . . ah, hhha, hhha!" Pam sobbed harder.

Pam snuffled and sobbed as Carol directed her to the '60s-style low-profile couch with burnt-orange upholstery. "Then what happened?" Carol prompted her.

"Then they . . . then they—" Pam could barely catch her breath. "They got the harness around the little girl . . . but . . . but she wouldn't let go of her . . . her *kitten*. . . ."

"She had a kitten?"

Pam nodded, unable to speak. Her face contorted as she soundlessly mouthed the words, "A wet little kitten." A new wave of tears rolled down her red cheeks as she snuffled and struggled to regain her composure.

"And they almost had her *in* the helicopter, but she started to slip out of the harness . . . and that's when Michael—dear poor, sweet Michael—leaned way out of the door to grab her. But he couldn't quite reach, so he unhooked his safety harness . . . and he caught her by one arm, still clinging to her little kitten, just as she started to fall—" Pam squeaked. She cried harder.

Carol rocked and held her sister in her arms and smoothed the hair on the top of her head for several minutes until finally Pam's breathing was almost normal again.

"Tell me what happened next," Carol said.

Her voice shaking, Pam continued, "It was pouring-down rain, and there was lightning crashing everywhere, and he caught her at the last possible moment and pulled her to safety with her still clinging to her little kitten. But just then, as the pilot pulled away, there was a strong gust of wind and the helicopter listed to one side—" Pam gestured the leaning helicopter with her hand "—and Michael started to *slip out the door*." Pam sobbed hard.

"Oh, dear *God*," Carol whispered sarcastically.

"The little girl screamed, and the winch operator reached out to grab him, but it was too late . . . and he fell!" Pam wailed and sobbed anew. "He fell . . . but he landed in some power lines. Oh, thank God the power was off, because there he was, laughing and smiling and waving, —you know the way Michael always does—and the pilot flew back around to drop him a line—"

"You want some coffee?" Carol asked, reaching for a box of Kleenex on the coffee table.

Pam waved her off and continued as Carol got up from the couch, set the Kleenex box next to her sister, and headed for the kitchen.

"Well . . . nobody knows how it happened," Pam continued, raising her voice so Carol could hear her in the kitchen, "but right then, the wire Michael was hanging onto just *snapped*! And the last anybody saw of him he was hanging onto the wire, swinging down to the ground—" Pam made a swooping motion with her arm "—and he crashed right into the side of the church and was *impaled* on the cross! Ahhhhhhh! Oh, my *God*! I loved him *so much*! What am I ever going to do?" Pam wailed.

"Poor Michael," Carol sighed, walking back to the living room with a soft drink in her hand instead of coffee. "This one's going to take some time to heal, honey. But you're strong. You're going to be all right."

"No, I won't!" Pam cried angrily, slapping the couch cushion with her hand.

"Yes, you *will*," Carol said flatly. "You can write a new character."

"Write a new character? Just like that? I can't just *write* a new character! There will *never* be another Michael!" Pam sobbed.

Carol held her sister in her arms and comforted her on the couch for several minutes and then said softly,

"There's Raoul. . . ."

"*Raoul*?" Pam squeaked.

Carol nodded. "Raoul."

"Who's Raoul?" Pam asked, wiping her nose on her sleeve.

"Oh, Pam, he's so good looking. And he's from Guatemala."

"Guatemala?" Pam sat up a little straighter and wiped the tears from her cheeks. She took the cold drink from Carol's hand and swallowed half of it in several loud, quick gulps.

"Oh, yes," Carol said. "And he graduated from Columbia University, and he's an investment banker, and he drives one of those new Tesla electric sports cars."

"An investment banker?"

"Yes! And he invests all his money in third-world sustainable farming projects—*and* earns his living installing wind farms off the coast of Denmark."

"Really . . . *Denmark*?" Pam said, hauling herself up off the couch to look in a mirror hanging in the hall.

"*Really*," Carol assured her.

Pam pinched her cheeks and smoothed her hair as she pondered her reflection. "I look *awful*," she said as she pulled at the bags under her red eyes with her fingers.

"Oh, you're going to be fine, baby," Carol said. "You'll be *just fine!*"

"Raoul. . . ." Pam said.

THE SUICIDE NOTE

Satisfied at last, he placed the smooth silver pen—the one she had given him on their second date—carefully on the desk next to the note. Numerous crumpled balls of French, Clairefontaine, ultra-smooth, bright-white, twenty-four-pound vellum, double-bleached, heavyweight, professional-grade writing paper lay scattered on the dusty wooden floor around his desk. The butt of a Pall Mall cigarette smoldered in the ashtray.

He lifted the heavy, large-caliber handgun and chambered a round. He pressed the cold, flat-black steel tight against his right temple. He glanced down and read the note one last time. He clicked the safety off. He took a final deep breath and held it. He closed his eyes, cleared his mind, and then. . . .

He clicked the safety back on with his thumb.

Still holding the gun to his head, he opened his eyes and read the note one last time. Focusing his attention on the page that lay squarely on the desk before him, he slowly moved the gun away from his head and set it gently on the heavy teak desk.

He read the note again.

"Please forgive me. . . ." it began.

Snarling like a cornered animal, he angrily snatched it up, crushed it in his trembling hands, and threw it across the empty room with an anguished grunt.

He sat motionless, staring out the dirty window of his dingy third-floor apartment.

He took the pen in his hand. It felt like the only friend he had left in the world. The gleaming, brushed stainless-steel surface, the perfect balance, the smooth glide of the medium blue ink ball. And he began to write, "By the time you read this . . ."

THE BROKEN HEART

The doctor listened carefully to my heart with his stethoscope.

"Is it broken?" I asked.

"No, it isn't broken," he replied. "It just feels like it's broken because someone you love is sad—and she is very far away—and you cannot be there to help her."

My eyes filled with tears.

"She'll be fine," he said. "She's a strong girl, and she loves you very much."

I stared at the floor as salty dewdrops fell from my eyes one by one.

"Your heart is only sprained," he said. "I know it feels broken, but if you stay off it for a few weeks it will mend. You have a good, strong heart that loves deeply, and in time it will be just like new."

I nodded. "I miss her terribly," I said.

"I know you do," he replied. "And she misses you as well. She will be fine—you both will be. Now go home and give your heart a rest. And come back to see me if it isn't better in a few weeks."

I nodded again, unable to speak, and left the exam room.

I cried as I wandered back toward my life without her. "This sure feels like a broken heart to me," I said quietly to the sidewalk passing beneath my feet.

WAITING FOR SPRING

From my little window I see the seasons changing,
and I long to visit places I have not been since summer
left with the green leaves to vacation on a warm southern
beach.

How strange and foreign it is to walk alone in my own
backyard.
The grass has grown too tall.
Fallen branches lie broken and forgotten since this
imprisonment.
This pain.
This weakness.

How familiar now, this small room.
These thoughts and walls, all papered in distant memories
of things that no longer matter.

The ticking clock measures the time I have left, and my
wanderlust waits, impatient and restless.

How I long to go with him.
To see new faces.
To learn new names.
To hear new stories.

In the cold, wet distance I hear passing cars,
and I wonder where their blurred wheels are taking them
and the smiling people inside.

"Fender bender? Move right," the sign says.
"Move right," the sign insists.
"Move right, and let the rest of the world rush past," the
sign commands.

Floundering helplessly in an ocean of chemically altered
senses,
I struggle toward mediocrity.
The bone-grinding damage to the underpinnings of my
body holds me like a drowning man to this chair.
I am unable to escape the locks and the chains that assure
my doom.

In my breathless panic I try to focus on the coming
spring—
through the end of fall and beyond all of winter.

Spring! I know that she is out there, beckoning me with
her gentle smile.

Wooing me with her sweet and distant song.

How I long for her.
To feel her warm flesh on my cheek . . . her breathless
kiss.

I stare out my little window and imagine her there,
waiting for me to heal so that I can come to her warm
embrace.

So that we can dance slow and loving in the warm night.
So that she can whisper in my ear, "I love you."

THE SHOEBOX

It was the middle of the winter of 1966 in Holland, Michigan. I was sixteen years old, and the only thing in life I was sure of, was that one day soon, I would fall down and die from acute boredom—without ever losing my virginity.

As I hunched through the front door of Fascano's Pizza to escape the late-January cold and stomped the snow off my boots, I scanned the room to see if anybody I knew was there—there wasn't.

I ordered the cheapest things on the menu at the front counter—breadsticks and a glass of water—then slunk to a red-vinyl booth and slid into its corner while I waited for the waitress to bring me my usual order.

Fascano's was on South River Avenue just at the edge of downtown Holland, and it was the local high school hangout. On this particular Wednesday it was still early, not long after dark, so none of my friends were there yet. Or, I should say, neither of my friends were there yet.

The place was so packed on weekends that you couldn't get a seat, but who would want to? After the game on Friday it was all jocks and cheerleaders. Unbearable. On Saturdays the place was jammed with squares and their families. Ugh. And on Sundays—just like every other business in the devoutly religious city of Holland—Fascano's was closed.

Monday through Thursday evenings though, Fascano's was where the hip and the attempting-to-be-hip hung out, at least until spring finally arrived and we could go back to hanging out on the sidewalk in front of the drugstore uptown or at Ottawa Beach State Park.

The only other hangout in Holland was the pool hall, but it was all greasers and gear heads, no chicks. You had to pay to be there so you could play pool. I never was any good at pool, so I just felt stupid playing the guys who practically lived there. They would rack the balls, drop them all before my first shot, and then I had to front another quarter before I could play again. My two-dollar-a-week allowance didn't go far in the pool hall.

At Fascano's I could occupy a booth for three or four hours with just breadsticks and water. Someone would inevitably show up and order something that would keep us in the booth until it was just too boring to sit there any longer, and we would either split up to go home, or hang out around Eighth Street, the main drag, and watch girls go by in cars until it got to be too damn cold.

The waitress brought my order and I sat up in my seat, sliding two quarters across the table. "Keep it," I said, referring to the ten-cents change she reached into her apron pocket for. She took my quarters and left without saying a word. She didn't even smile. I gave her a twenty-percent tip. What she didn't know was that the ten cents I gave her was twenty percent of my entire life savings.

I dipped my middle finger into the glass of water and traced it around the lip of the glass. Carefully unfolding a paper napkin from the chrome dispenser on the table, I gently laid it across the top of the water glass as smoothly as I could. The thin paper clung to the wet rim, and I pulled the remainder of the napkin down over the glass, leaving a paper drumhead attached to the lip.

I dug into the pocket of my surplus military field jacket and found a soft pack of Old Gold cigarettes. I took one out, lit it, and took a long first drag then slouched back into the corner of the booth with my legs crossed on the vinyl cushion.

With an artist's concentration I twirled the ash of my cigarette on the edge of a gold-aluminum ashtray to make the glowing end into a point and began burning little holes in the paper one at a time.

This was a game everyone played at Fascano's. Anywhere from two to six people would take turns burning the smallest hole possible in the paper until the center broke off and fell into the water. The last person to burn was the loser. This was not a game for winners.

Practicing my smoking technique and my water glass game was an ideal way to pass the time until something happened—*anything*.

An hour had crawled by, maybe longer, when Larry Nichols and Pete Fowler appeared at the door. They hustled inside, pushed along by a gust of wind and a flurry of snow, and loitered around the front counter waiting for someone to see them so they could order something, but then Larry saw me. He said something to Pete, and they came over to my booth.

I hardly noticed the cardboard shoebox Pete had tucked under his left arm. Larry, a kid who walked without ever touching his heels to the ground, had his hands stuffed into the pockets of his Navy pea coat.

Pete did a quick hair toss then slid into my booth opposite me, placing the shoebox on the table as he did. Larry eased in next to him. Neither of them said anything; they just sat there and looked at me expressionlessly, like they had just knocked over a liquor store or something.

Pete slid the shoebox to the middle of the table so that it was directly between us and held the top of the box with both hands. He slowly raised the lid just enough so that I could get a good look inside.

"Fuuuuuck . . . !" I said. "Where the hell did you get *that*?"

"I got it," Pete said without a hint of emotion in his voice. He slammed the top shut and slid the box off the table, setting it next to him on the red vinyl. He folded his hands on the table and turned to look at Larry.

Taking his cue, Larry dug and fumbled and pulled at the pocket of his pea coat until he finally produced the latest advancement in slingshot technology, the coveted and elusive Wrist Rocket. A single piece of tubular aluminum, machine bent into the perfectly shaped frame, with strong surgical tubing for propulsion, and this one was even cooler because it looked brand new and was finished in gleaming, dark-blue metal-flake paint.

Larry put the device on the table and said nothing. Trying not to show my envy, I casually admired the piece and skeptically touched its black molded-plastic handgrip. Knowing exactly what my next move was going to be, I didn't flinch. I made 'em sweat.

They waited intently for me to be impressed, but it was my turn to impress them. I calmly reached into the pocket of my well-worn, bell-bottomed, hip-hugger blue jeans and pulled out the keys to my father's three-year-old, 1963 Pontiac Catalina two-door coupe. A two-tone—metallic cadet blue with a white top, three-speed automatic transmission and a 389 cubic-inch mill with a four-barrel carb under the hood.

I dangled the keys in front of Larry and Pete suggestively for a second or two then dropped them with a clunk on the table next to the slingshot. Nobody moved.

Larry reached for the keys, but before he could get to them I snatched them back and spun them in their key fob on my finger. We exchanged glances for a split second then simultaneously leaped from the booth and headed for the door.

We burst out onto the snowy sidewalk. Without saying a word, barely looking to see if there was any oncoming traffic, and darted across River Avenue to the parking lot on the other side.

"Shotgun!" Larry shouted as we jumped the curb in front of the car. Pete, who was a few steps behind, stomped his foot in anger at having to concede the right front seat but continued without further protest. I opened the driver's door and held the seat forward for him as he flipped his hair from his eyes, ducked his head, and climbed into the back.

As if escaping a bank heist, I fired up the Pontiac and spun the tires in reverse. Before the car stopped moving I dropped it into drive and gassed it just a little. The positraction rear end swung around as smooth as could be, and we were headed for the exit. I momentarily glanced both ways as we slid out onto the icy, hard-packed, snow-covered street, and then throttled it hard, opening the four-barrel carburetor that made a throaty hot-rod sound.

I power-slid the car perfectly sideways for half a block before performing a flawless recovery just in time to make the stop sign at the end of the block.

Larry and Pete didn't so much as budge. We may as well have been on our way to church with our parents in the car. Larry lit a cigarette and tapped it on the open ashtray between us. I idled the car at the stop sign for a long moment, thinking. I didn't have a clue as to where we were going, but Pete had at least a hundred M-80 firecrackers in that shoebox, Larry had a Wrist Rocket, and the Pontiac had a full tank of gas.

I turned up the radio and the announcer said, "It's *seven* o'clock Chicago, and this is *W-C-F-L*, the *voice* of the *Windy* City!" then cut to a commercial break.

We cruised out of town on South Shore Drive, listening to WCFL loud on the radio. WLS was the station that played the Top 40 but we liked WCFL because we could occasionally hear some Cream, Procol Harem, or Hendrix. Psychedelic music was brand new to those of us who were desperately trying to be hip. We all so wanted to be part of that scene. We idolized the very *idea* of being hip. In truth we were very far from it with our acne and peach-fuzz faces but we did everything we could to make up for our total lack of cool, which mostly meant listening to the right music—and WCFL played it.

Pete said we should go pucker-running, a term we used to describe going eighty miles an hour down one-lane, sandy, dirt-farm roads east of Holland, sliding around corners and splashing through mud puddles in the summer or blasting through headlight-high snow drifts in the winter. It was great fun if you had a beater and didn't mind hitting a tree now and then, but this was my dad's nice car, and I wasn't sure pucker-running was such a good idea.

Larry wanted to go to Saugatuck. He said there was this chick there, Marsha, who had some Seagram's Seven and with that, the decision was made. I headed toward Saugatuck twenty-three miles due south along the lakeshore.

As we got close to the end of South Shore Drive, out where the rich people lived, I pulled into the parking lot of the Central Park Reformed Church—a place I occasionally drove girls to make out—and we all got out to piss.

Getting back in the car, Larry joined Pete in the backseat and said, "Let's take the Beeline."

The Beeline was the name of a rutted and potholed secondary road that went straight south toward Saugatuck, a shortcut if you drove it faster than a responsible driver would.

I hung a left onto the road that would become the Beeline and take us out through the ancient Lake Michigan sand dunes and eventually to Saugatuck Dunes State Park. I figured we would go up into the dunes at the park to shoot off the M-80s. Huge, commercial-grade firecrackers the size and shape of shotgun shells that went off like a hand grenade when you lit the short green fuse that stuck out of the red paper body on the side. Like a toy-sized stick of dynamite, an M-80 was one of the most dangerous items a brainless and bored sixteen-year-old male could possess. Also high on that list was the Wrist Rocket, advertised as a hunting-grade slingshot; it had as much firepower as a spring-loaded pellet gun but could fire anything from small rocks to ball bearings. An M-80 and a powerful slingshot were a truly dangerous combination . . . and we had both.

I'd heard that some guys used M-80s for fishing. All you had to do was row out into a lake, toss a couple of M-80s into the water, and scoop up the dead fish. It saved a lot of time and bait. Farmers kept them around to throw at deer that came to nibble gardens. I couldn't begin to imagine where Pete had got a whole shoebox full of them. All I knew was that I had only seen one M-80 go off in my life. It made my ears ring for a whole day after Jimmy Peterson lit it on the back of his brother's flatbed truck. That was the first time I had ever felt the concussion of anything that big going off—and Jimmy and I were fifteen feet away.

Not two miles beyond the Holland city limits, roaring down the snow-covered road, I heard the sound of the back window going down. I looked in the rear-view mirror and saw Pete and Larry huddled together doing something. There were a few seconds of action back there, then a bright-white flash and an explosion of snow on the side of the road behind the car. The guys screamed and laughed with delight and immediately began preparing another shot.

I took my foot off the gas, and the Pontiac slowed as we approached a roadside mailbox. Pete held the Wrist Rocket at the ready, aiming forward out the rear passenger window. Larry lit the fuse, Pete launched the paper grenade, and it flew toward the mailbox, its sparkling fuse arcing through the darkness, exploding just over the top of the mailbox as we zoomed past. The noise was deafening. The guys cheered and slapped at each other in the backseat. Speeding into the snowy winter darkness, rock music blaring, and yelling at the top of our lungs, we headed for the next roadside target believing we had just invented the most fun game on the planet.

As the miles flew past we perfected our strategy, but it didn't take long for the combination of fifteen-degree weather and forty-mile-an-hour speed to take its toll on our fingers and cheeks, so the guys would roll the electric window down for each launch then back up again once the deed had been done.

The combined action of putting an M-80 into the sling of the Wrist Rocket, pulling back the surgical tubing, rolling down the window and, at the precise moment, lighting the fuse, releasing the projectile, and ducking as the explosive blast lit up the night took on a military-like choreography of collaboration in the backseat that was the coolest shit ever.

Fishtailing the Pontiac down the road, I would scout out the perfect target, alert my crew, slow to the correct speed, move the car into proper alignment with the objective, yell "Fire!" then floor the gas pedal just as the explosion took place.

We were getting pretty good after not much practice at all. Pete got one to land inside a mailbox that had no door and blew it to pieces. The shot was so well placed that we had to stop and get out of the car and dance around in the snow for as long as we could stand the bitter cold.

Getting back in, Larry insisted on getting the window seat and a chance to fire the Wrist Rocket, but by that time we were pretty far out into the countryside, halfway to Saugatuck, and there were few houses . . . and even fewer roadside targets.

Anticipation nearly gave way to boredom as I looked for a sign of civilization that would provide the next level of adrenaline-pumping thrill. Larry was anxious to get his first shot off so he could try to outdo Pete's crescendo of drive-by vandalism.

Then, there at the furthest reaches of the headlights I saw a large mailbox. Made of wood, it was built to look like a farm tractor. This was the target we had been looking for all night but we hadn't, until this moment, known exactly what that might be.

"Check it out!" I yelled over the sound of The Box Tops singing "The Letter," pointing at the front of the car.

"Holy shit!" came the refrain from the back seat. Larry's voice was still changing, and he accidentally yelled a little too loud and ended up squealing like a ten-year-old girl. "Get ready! Get ready!" he commanded in his girlish squeak.

Larry grabbed an M-80 from the shoebox and situated it in the Wrist Rocket and pulled back hard on the surgical tubing. Acting quickly, Pete lit the fuse, but Larry fumbled the window control with his gloved finger while trying to hold the Wrist Rocket steady and roll down the window at the same time. He lost his grip on the M-80 just as the window began to open. The explosive released prematurely.

In seemingly slow motion, with all the power the Wrist Rocket had to offer, the projectile flew less than a foot and struck the headliner just above the window opening. From there, it ricocheted up and back and hit the middle of the roof just above the front seat back, then bounced into the open shoebox containing the rest of the M-80s.

The fuses in the box instantly began to ignite, and the back seat area of the car started to fill with smoke.

Pete leaped over the seat into the front screaming, "Stop the car! Stop the car!"

Larry squealed unintelligibly from the back seat as he scrambled to free himself from the Wrist Rocket, get the window down, and jump out.

I slammed on the brakes, but the car seemed to pick up speed as the tires slid along the snow-covered road. I pulled at the handle of the door and tried to open it, but we were still going too fast, and the wind kept me inside. The car began to slide sideways as I tried to correct, but it was no use.

In full panic mode, I jammed the emergency brake with my left foot. The car continued to slide. I threw the shift lever into park just as the first M-80 went off with a deafening roar. Larry fell out the back window. Pete got the passenger door open and leaped out onto the road. I hesitated another second, still trying to stop the car, then bailed out just as the entire shoebox in the back seat began to go off.

The car slid a few more feet and came to rest in the middle of the road, its headlights pointing into the woods. We ran as far and as fast as we could as the M-80 explosions went rapidly from one at a time, to several at a time, to what sounded like a single, long, drawn-out, night-shattering cacophony of full-scale warfare all going off at once. There must have been seventy or eighty of them left. I plugged my ears with my fingers and watched in horror as the car lit up like the Fourth of July from within, and smoke began to billow from the open doors and the back window.

When the explosions finally subsided and we were pretty sure the last one had gone off, an orange glow began to emanate from the heavily smoking car in the middle of the road ten yards away. I rushed to the car and began throwing snow inside as quickly as I could.

"Help me! Help me!" I screamed.

The guys ran up and joined me, and in under a minute we'd managed to put out the fire that had been burning on the backseat and in the headliner. Blackened seat springs smoldered where the box of M-80s had been, and burned seat stuffing and wet red paper was everywhere in the car. The interior light had melted when the headliner caught fire; a long string of plastic hung from the fixture. A crust of black melted plastic interior light cover, oozed down the seat back. My heart was racing. I thought I was going to throw up. My father was going kill me, no question about it.

Merrilee Rush sang "Angel of the Morning" on the radio while we cleaned as much soggy cardboard, burned headliner, red paper, and snow as we possibly could from the back of the car. And when we had done all we possibly could, we three silently climbed into the front seat. I turned off the radio, made a U-turn in the road, and headed toward home.

We didn't listen to WCFL. We didn't talk. We just smoked cigarettes, warmed our hands on the dashboard vents, and rode in silence with all the windows down to try to get rid of the smell of burned foam rubber and spent gunpowder.

It was well past midnight by the time I dropped off the guys. On the street in front of Larry's house, I spent some more time picking bits of burned seat and red paper off the floor and the rear window deck of the car.

As slowly as I could, I coasted the car into the driveway and turned off the ignition before it came to a complete stop. I got out of the Pontiac and closed the door gently with a single click of the latch.

That was when I noticed the white paint of the roof, burned black and blistered in a large circle in the middle of the once pristine body. I felt my knees go weak. I felt a surge of adrenaline, and my heart began to pound as the consequences of the night became apparent to me.

I let myself in the front door and tiptoed up the stairs to my room, and for the remainder of the night and into the early gray light of morning, I lay in my bed staring at the ceiling, knowing that the coming day would surely be my last.

I heard my stepmother shuffle to the kitchen downstairs to scramble my father's eggs. The clock ticked on my bedside table. I heard them talking quietly downstairs as he ate his breakfast.

I heard my father go out the front door, heard the storm door close behind him as he stepped off the porch.

Imagining the worst nightmare of my life, that was about to take place, I clenched my eyes shut and held my breath.

What came next sounded like an echo from across the street—the unmistakable sound of my father's voice as he screamed, "*Je-sus* Fucking Christ!"

I heard him throw open the storm door, slam the front door behind him, march through the living room, and stomp up the stairs to my room.

I knew I was about to be in the deepest shit I had ever been in—*by far*. My bedroom door burst open, and my father rushed in screaming, "WHAT . . . in the

GODDAMMED *HELL* . . . happened to my . . . GODDAMMED CAR?"

I stared at his bulging eyes, his clenched jaw, and his balled fists. I couldn't speak. I swallowed hard and began to sit up in bed, trying to convey calm.

I didn't have a second to think about my next words. "We were struck by lightning," I blurted out.

"WHAT?"

"We were struck by lightning," I repeated. Expecting to be pummeled to death in the next moment, I cowered.

My father didn't say anything. He just stared at me intently, veins bulging from his neck and forehead, for what seemed like eternity as he tried to make sense of what I had just told him. He was wholly unprepared for that answer or anything remotely like it.

He relaxed a little, and I took a shallow breath.

"Who was with you?" he asked more calmly now.

"Pete and Larry."

His anger turned to concern. "Is everyone okay?"

"My ears are still ringing."

"I don't doubt it. Are the guys all right?"

"I guess so. . . ." I said, "I dropped them off."

"Did you get any sleep?"

"No, not much." I lied. I hadn't so much as blinked my eyes for the previous six hours.

"Well, you better get some sleep." He said.

He came to my bedside and seated himself next to me. He rubbed my head. "Are you sure you're okay?" he asked.

"I was worried about your car."

"Aw, fuck the car. I'm just glad you're okay." He hugged me, then kissed me on my forehead and got up to leave. He turned to look at me as he closed my door quietly, and I heard him creak down the stairs.

I listened to him telling my stepmother what had happened as a single tear rolled down each side of my face.

I heard my stepmother exclaim something, and then I heard my father say, "He's okay, he's okay. Thank God, he's okay."

Thankful to be alive, I rolled onto my stomach, buried my face into my pillow, and cried hard. I cried because I felt so bad about what had happened to my father's beautiful car. I cried because it was so awful to have lied to him about it. And I cried because the one thing in my life that I was sure of was that one person in the world loved me—very, very much.

That afternoon a tow truck came and hauled my father's ruined Pontiac away.

We had a new rented station wagon for a few weeks after that, and one day my father drove into the driveway with his Pontiac sparkling as good as new.

We checked it carefully together. Aside from it looking much newer than it had before and the lingering smell of fresh paint, we both agreed we couldn't tell anything had ever happened.

We moved away from Michigan the following summer. The last time I saw Larry and Pete they were sitting around a table at Fascano's with a bunch of their friends, and Pete was entertaining them all by imitating shooting something with a Wrist Rocket. Those guys must have told that story a hundred times. It was just so fucking cool.

Not more than a season before my father died, I did finally tell him the truth—all of it, every detail—while having dinner with him more than thirty years later, in the dining room of his little apartment, in the little town of Issaquah Washington, sharing some seafood linguine we had made together.

He laughed out loud as I told him the story and he shook his head grinning, as he poured both of us a little more wine.

When my confession was finally finished and the evening had grown late, and it was time for me to go, my father held me in his arms a little longer than usual as I said goodbye. He patted me on my back and gave me a brusque kiss on my neck, and said quietly, "You know, years ago, Pete Fowler's dad told me the same story."

IF

If I.
If we.
Were to . . .

It would be because you, as usual, would stand too close.

And she would sing to us, all soft and smooth,
her voice oozing out of the speakers like warm cream,
her music flowing into the room like spilled syrup.
We would feel the music, barely audible over the beating
of our hearts.
The music, the mark and measure of the union of our
souls.
Our hearts keeping time and rhythm with her song.
The soft, quiet music surrounding us, we we'd rock
together slowly.
We would feel the flow. We would dance in place.

I would smell your scent. I would feel your breath.
I 'd move my mouth close to yours.

I would feel your life on my skin.

I 'd hesitate for just a moment then kiss your upper lip.
Taste you with my tongue. Hold you in my arms.
Hold you—close and loving.

We'd linger in the moment and savor the languid
breathlessness, the childish excitement of togetherness.

I would trace your neck with the back of my finger and
guide your swaying hips.
Gently, softly, barely touching, breathing in your special
scent,
I would kiss you on your mouth.
I would offer you my closeness.
You would feel my warmth and strength.

And she would sing to us so sweetly.
We would move and sway with her song.
I would feel the warmth of your body;
your heartbeat in rhythm with mine.

THEY CRIED

They always cry when I do something for them. This is how I know for sure they actually need a little help. The old man trying to scrape together enough money to rent a room at the cheap motel down the street so he can sleep out of the pouring rain. The old black woman standing outside the Safeway store late at night asking for enough change to catch the bus home to Seattle. When I look them in the eye and speak directly to them. When I give them what they need instead of what little they are asking for. When they are actually looking for just a little help and aren't trying to scam someone for the next drink or the next fix but really have nothing, not even something to eat, it's always the same. They always cry.

This time it was a pair of plain-looking women in an old, white box van that appeared to contain their combined lives' possessions. I was pumping gas for my work truck when they showed up at the station and pulled in behind me.

I casually watched as they went through their purses and pockets, and finally one of them got out of the truck and went inside carrying three one-dollar bills and some change.

She was the older of the two, wearing an oversized t-shirt and blue jeans. She seemed to be in charge, the one who knew what needed to be done. The one who tried her best not to let her friend know just how dire their situation was.

After a minute or two she came out of the store waving, and the other woman pumped a little over a gallon of gas into the tank. Then they both climbed back into the van and prepared to leave.

I could tell by their actions and the looks on their faces they were not having a real good day.

Engaged in serious and quiet conversation, they didn't see me as I went to the driver's window.

"Did you just put three dollars in your tank?" I asked.

"Yeah, why?" the driver replied with just a hint of skepticism in her voice.

"How about if I put a little more in there for you?" I waved my credit card.

"Oh, my God," the driver said. She looked a little stunned.

The other woman looked on concerned.

"If you hold on for a minute," I said, "I'll put another twenty in there for you." As I went to the pay station and entered my card and my numbers I saw them speaking to each other in quiet disbelief.

"What are you ladies doing today?" I asked cheerily as I pumped.

The driver stepped out of the van and said, "We're looking for a place to live. The place we were living turned out to be kind of a nightmare, so we're on our way to get the last of her stuff. Then it looks like the old van here is home for a while." She put on a brave face and gave the side of the faded old truck a gentle pat.

"I'm not going to just give you free gas, you know," I said. "You have to listen to me tell you a story."

"Okay," she said, smiling skeptically, not quite knowing what to expect. She tried to smooth her hair a little with her fingers.

As I filled their tank, I told her about how my daughter had been in a serious car accident during a blizzard and that a Good Samaritan had stopped to help her and had driven her to a hospital many miles away then checked her into a motel and had stayed with her for more than a whole day until her mother could come to take her home.

I told her about how, because of this, I had made a solemn vow to be a better man and to help people wherever and whenever I could and that I was living up to that solemn personal vow at this very moment.

"Oh, my God," she said, her eyes filling with tears, "you're paying it forward."

"Not really," I said, trying to hold back my own tears. "It's more like I'm paying it back."

I smiled and went back to pumping gas well beyond the twenty bucks I had promised. She watched the numbers on the gas pump spin by and whispered to her friend through the window.

I saw wiping away her tears but looked away so I wouldn't embarrass her. I focused my attention on pumping gas and tried not to think about the impact I was having on this woman and her friend. I watched the passing traffic and tried to predict the coming storm as dark clouds rolled in the distance as the uncomfortable moments of silence between us ticked by, marked by the sound of the gas pump.

Her companion had been writing something in the van. She got out on the passenger's side and came around to where we were standing just behind the driver's door.

I topped off the tank, making sure it was completely full, and as I put the nozzle back on the gas pump she handed me a scrap of paper and said, "I wrote this for you."

The note read:

Trina and Sandy. She had written her phone number. *Let us cook for you or something sometime. Thanks so much. I needed to meet someone real here. It's so lonely here. Thanks. God bless you. Trina.*

I read the note and smiled and then screwed their gas cap back on.

As I turned to go Sandy asked, "Can I give you a hug?"

"Sure," I said. I let her take me in her arms.

"Thank you so much," she cried. She held me tightly for a moment or two. When she released me, Trina took me in her arms and sobbed into my neck without saying anything.

"You have to give us your number so we can pay you back," Sandy said.

"No," I said. "One day when you can afford it, pay it back to someone who really needs it. Do it in my honor the same as I am doing this in someone else's honor."

"We will, we will," Sandy whispered, wiping tears from her cheeks.

Trina nodded and put an arm over Sandy's shoulder, "Thank you so much," she said.

"No, thank you," I said. "Thank you for allowing me to honor someone who taught me a great deal. And thank you for helping me to become a better man."

I walked a few paces back to my truck and watched as they got in their van, wiping tears from their faces.

I gave them a short wave and drove away.

I have still not forgotten my vow. To be a better man, to try to change the world one good deed at a time and to honor the woman who rescued my child and changed my life forever. They always cry when I do something like this, and they always want to hug me. I am always reminded of why I am doing it. And I always cry, too.

THE ER DOCTOR

In her tight-fitting, flower-print maroon hospital scrubs, she was one of the most attractive women he had seen in a very long time. He'd caught a glimpse of a small, deep-violet streak in her silky brown hair a moment earlier, but he couldn't see that just now as her physician's ID badge and perfect breasts were exactly at eye level and directly in front of him.

She plucked through what little was left of his charred hair and scrutinized the damage to his scalp under a bright, overhead examination light.

As she worked on him, he sat upright on the edge of the hospital bed and stared point blank at her magnificent figure, savoring the faint white ginger scent of her expensive designer perfume.

"What made you run back in?" she asked as she worked.

"What?"

"Why did you go back into a burning building?"

She stopped dabbing antiseptic cream on the exposed areas of his head to look at him.

"I didn't go back in. I was already in there."

She stood back from him a few inches. "Why didn't you get out when you saw that your apartment was on fire?"

"I guess I didn't notice," he said, wanting her to go back to what she had been doing so that he could continue to feel the softness of her thigh as she leaned against his leg.

"You didn't notice that your apartment was fully engulfed in flames?"

"No, not really."

"Did you notice that your hair had caught fire and your scalp was burning?" she asked with a note of sarcasm in her voice.

"Yes, of course I did. That's when I got the hell out of there."

She went back to tending the first- and second-degree burns on his head. She dropped a piece of sooty gauze onto a stainless-steel tray and plucked a new one from a blue paper package lying open on the portable instrument tray next to his bed.

"Your hair will probably eventually grow back," she said, "but in the meantime you should wear a hat and stay out of the sun."

She squirted some antiseptic liquid onto the new gauze pad and leaned against his body—a little more than she had before—and worked her way down the back of his head. He was at the same moment in excruciating pain and unworldly ecstasy as she nearly pressed her breasts into his face. She worked in silence and plucked a scrap of burnt shirt collar from the back of his neck with a pair of tweezers.

"This is going to blister," she said nonchalantly.

He didn't respond.

"I'll write you a prescription for some pain medication when we're through here," she continued.

His heart fluttered as he thought about her penning a prescription for him. He imagined her on a movie set, writing a prescription in slow motion, those long fingers wrapped around a gleaming, brushed stainless-steel ballpoint pen. He thought he might be experiencing a little pain-induced shock, but the tingle between his legs dismissed that notion.

"So what were you doing that you didn't notice that your place was on fire?"

"I was writing," he said.

She froze. She moved away from him so she could look him straight in the eye. "Did you say you were . . . *writing?*"

"Yes."

"You're a *writer?*" There was a hint of excitement in her voice.

"Yes, I am."

"Oh, my *God,*" She paused, staring directly at his eyes. "What do you write?"

"Right now? I'm working on some flash fiction."

"Flash fiction? I *love* flash fiction! My favorite Ernest Hemingway story was flash fiction!"

"The one about the baby shoes . . . six words," he said.

"Yes!" she said. "I cried." She momentarily covered her mouth with her hand as she recalled the emotion brought by Hemingway's words.

Attempting to regain her stoic professionalism, she gave him a shot of morphine. "This will help ease the pain for a few hours," she said, stabbing him in the thigh with a syringe. She carefully wrapped his head in a gauze bandage while he languished in the rapture of morphine. They laughed and joked together over every line of the aftercare information sheet, critiquing it for grammatical correctness and punctuation.

"There's no inciting incident!" he exclaimed.

"Where's the focal character's motivation?" she demanded.

They howled with laughter. She touched him on the arm several times as they shared life stories, and she committed every snippet of his personal life to memory. When she had checked his blood pressure again, taken his temperature, and palpitated all of his major organs and could think of no further reason not to release him from the emergency room she asked, "Do you have a ride home?"

"No. I came in an ambulance."

She nodded and looked at him solemnly. "Is there a home left for you to go to?"

Tears began to well in his eyes as he came to grips with the loss of all of his most recent short stories and poetry, the only things in the world that mattered to him. To avoid the embarrassment of crying, he simply shook his bandaged head.

She looked at her watch. "*Well,*" she said, "isn't that coincidental? *You're* my last patient! My shift ended about twenty minutes after they brought you in here. I'll tell you what, since you've been such a good patient, I'll drive you anywhere you'd like to go. They probably wouldn't let you on a bus looking like that anyway."

He thought about her offer for a long moment.

"Do you have somewhere you can go?" she asked.

"How about your place?"

She caught her breath. "I would love that," she said huskily, brushing a stray hair from her face with her hand. "You wait here. I'll be right back. I just need to clock out." She swung the privacy curtain closed as she left the room.

He untied the hospital gown he was wearing and reached for his smoke-blackened clothes. '*Everything's gonna' be okay,*' he thought to himself. '*This is going to be great material.*'

EXTRAORDINARY AWARENESS

Yesterday, driving alone, attending to my business, I saw something in the road. I turned my head as I passed it, attempting to verify its origins. My natural curiosity was aroused.

I travel more than most people and often see things lying in the road that others might miss. I have on occasion stopped or turned around to get a better look and, on occasion, the item has turned out to be treasure of some sort. I have found wallets, purses left on the roofs of cars, and once a fat bundle of cash wrapped in a rubber band. I have been told once or twice, by persons of insight—people who would know such things—that I have "extraordinary awareness."

Upon first meeting me, psychics, mystics, and palm readers alike will often raise their eyebrows at me and exclaim, "Now, *this* is interesting . . ."

And at the end of whatever session I'm participating in, whether social or professional, people of wisdom and mysticism always take the time to tell me that extraordinary awareness is their conclusion.

I have always seen it as unusual curiosity more than awareness, and so it was not at all unusual for me this day to halt my mighty vehicle so that I might more closely examine that which lay before me, there in the road, glinting in the late afternoon sun, beckoning my scrutiny.

I stepped out. I turned back and jogged in the tall grass covered in late autumn leaves alongside the wet asphalt to see what the thing actually was.

The closer I got the more conflicted I became. The early realization of what I was seeing made me even more determined to confirm my expectation.

Breathing heavily, I slowed my pace so as to get a better view. I checked for traffic. None. I rushed out to get a closer look. I was momentarily conflicted.

How could this be? Was this some kind of sign from the universe?

I stared intently at the item, trying to get some sense of its meaning. Was it a message of some kind? Had it been intentionally placed for me to find? Or . . . was it a simple twist of fate?

I looked both ways, standing in the middle of an otherwise unoccupied roadway, and experienced great consternation as I tried to make a decision.

There could be no mistake; I had to do something. I needed to take bold and decisive action. It was a cathartic moment that held great meaning for me, but I could find no obvious course.

I just couldn't decide. There, lying at my feet, a gleaming stainless reflection in the brilliant afternoon sunlight, so utilitarian in its form and function, so simple and yet so complicated, it was the one thing I had least expected to find in a road.

A fork.

THE PREDATOR

He reached beside his seat, and his hand naturally found a large metal lever with a motorcycle-style handle on the end. He twisted it easily, and as he did the engine speed began to increase. He gently pulled the handle up as he twisted. The helicopter began to vibrate rhythmically as the blades roared over his head, and then it lifted off. Just a couple of feet at first, but as the engine spun faster, the helicopter slowly rose, ten feet, then thirty, now a hundred.

With his right hand on the control between his legs and his left resting on the throttle, he barely moved the control stick forward—not more than a fraction of an inch—and as the powerful machine rose, it gently leaned in the direction he pointed and began to fly. Knowing his feet should be somewhere, they found the matching tail-rotor control pedals and rested gently on them. He pushed ever so lightly with his toes, first his right foot, then his left, and found that he could determine the direction he was facing by which way he pushed the pedals. He'd never flown a helicopter but it felt so natural; it was almost as though he could think the direction he wanted to go, and the machine would follow his mental command.

There ahead of him was the ocean and a long stretch of white sand beach as he continued to climb high above the palm trees. He glanced out the blue-tinted canopy at the cloudless sky above him. A small green mountain sprinkled with black lava rock boulders and bare patches of red dirt swung into view as he leaned left. He tugged at the control stick ever so slightly, watching the altimeter on the dashboard spin slowly clockwise as he rose gently above its craggy ridge, and then he headed for the lush, green tropical forests beyond.

He flew over the peak of the mountain, and the helicopter began to pitch and roll violently. It dropped and bounced in the turbulence of the ocean trade winds rushing over the hilltop. His heart pounded hard as he pulled on the stick and leaned back in his seat, willing the aircraft to rise above the danger. The fear of losing control of the powerful machine and crashing into the cliff below woke him from the dream suddenly.

He opened his eyes and became aware of where he really was and realized that the turbulence he was feeling was really just her climbing into bed on top of him.

Kneeling on the expensive goose-down comforter over his legs. She was amazingly gorgeous: that long, dark-brown hair, those milk chocolate eyes. Happy to be awake and thankful to be alive, knowing he wouldn't crash into a mountainside after all, he smiled at her.

"Good morning, beautiful," he said, looking directly at her ample breasts beneath the coat she was wearing. He wondered if that was all she was wearing.

After all the time and effort he'd put onto convincing her to go out with him, she'd really thrown him a curve ball when she agreed to go home with him. It didn't matter that she had so sternly insisted on sleeping on the couch in the living room, because now she sat upright on his legs and tossed her hair from one shoulder to the other; he loved it when she did that. He's seen her do it a hundred times.

He was very aware of his morning arousal as it lay almost touching his navel and wondered if she was going to notice it as well. Maybe she would finally do something about it. He wanted to show it to her, but he assumed she knew it was there. If she didn't . . . she would soon. He was also becoming aware that she had tied his hands to the bedpost, one on either side of his head. '*This*,' he thought, '*is going to be cool!*'

She smiled at him and brought her right hand from behind the small of her back, holding a large caliber, semi-automatic pistol that she pointed at his chest. With a slight grimace she pulled hard on the big steel slide, chambering a round and cocking the hammer. She tipped the gun slightly to one side and checked to be sure a bullet was visible then released the slide.

It slammed forward with a loud metallic clack.

He laughed inappropriately as he tried to make sense of what was happening; was this some kind of really cool morning sex game? He smiled at her and said, "Oh, baby, you're so bad. There's nothing sexier than a heavily armed woman."

Holding the big pistol with both hands, her right index finger resting on the trigger, her thumbs overlapping each other on the embossed rubber grip, she first pointed the matte-black gun at his face. He tried to move to push the gun away but she had tied him up with a pair of his best neckties, and the harder he pulled, the tighter the knots became. Still thinking she was playing with him, he didn't put up much of a struggle after realizing there really was no escape.

She pointed the gigantic bore of the barrel at his heart then dragged it down the length of his torso until it rested near the tip of his now rapidly shrinking manhood. She clicked the safety off with her right thumb, and her casually gentle gaze became an empty and angry glare. Her eyes narrowed, her lips tightened.

His hair tingled with electricity, and his eyes widened.

"So, tell me," she said, sounding for all the world like a well-seasoned cop interrogating a suspect, "how many times has this stalking thing worked for you in the past?"

SMUT

She dropped the manuscript heavily onto the old, hollow-core, mahogany bedroom door that served as his desk.

The door had been slammed so many times the latch was splintered beyond useable service, and on one side there was a fist-sized hole, the long forgotten reminder of a drunken woman's scorn. The door lay across a ramshackle stack of used cinder blocks and was leveled flat with a coverless dictionary and an old family bible.

A casual observer could see that the hinge-less relic was dark brown, but beyond that, there wasn't enough of it visible under the avalanche of papers, bills, books, pill bottles, dirty dishes, coffee cups, and a pint-size bottle of Bombay gin to identify it as a door.

Standing over him with her hands on her hips in those loose-fitting button-fly 501 Levi's with the legs turned up at the cuff, she looked angry . . . or disappointed. He couldn't tell which.

"What did you think?" he asked.

"Smut!" she declared.

The sparkle of those perfect white teeth behind her natural-pink lipstick lips captured his attention almost as much as the single word she barked at him.

There was a long silence between them as she paced to his side of the desk, dragging the copy by one corner along the perimeter of the old door, causing a landslide of papers and junk to rustle to the floor below.

"Cheap . . . guttural . . . worthless . . . lousy . . . *smut*," she said as she walked until she was standing over him.

He was crestfallen.

"I loved it," she continued, kicking off her patent-leather pumps and sliding out of her expensive, tailored blazer, revealing the cream silk camisole she wore beneath.

Tossing her reading glasses aside, she seated herself on his lap, burying his face with her mane of hair and whispered into his neck, "You *really* have a way with words—don't you?"

THE SUPERHERO

We were southbound on Highway 447 at eighty-five miles per hour a few miles out of Empire, Nevada, an ugly little convenience store of a town with a declining population of a hundred or so lonesome souls.

We'd been living in hot, dusty tents on Black Rock Desert for eight days, but now we were headed back to Reno, a hundred nine miles away, for more food, water, and gas. Heat waves on the blistering asphalt became a mirage of shimmering chrome on the distant horizon.

I wondered why she wasn't talking to me. Something wasn't right.

"So, what's going on?" I finally asked, turning to look at her as razor-sharp boulders and dead-brown scrub sagebrush whizzed past in the distance beyond her window.

"Nothing." She said. There was no emotion in her voice. She didn't appear angry or sad or anything, just vacant; as though wired to a lie detector and not telling the truth.

I let her drive on in silence. Hoping that whatever was so very wrong in her life had nothing to do with me. She was an adult now and she had earned the right to have feelings, whatever they were.

A ticket to Burning Man had been her high school graduation present from me, and this was her tenth consecutive annual trip to the playa. Burning Man takes place on Black Rock Desert in northern Nevada, a seven hundred-square-mile dry lake bed of flat, baked clay prone to years without rainfall, extreme and rapid temperature changes, and sixty mile per hour sustained windstorms that can last minutes, hours, or weeks.

A couple of decades earlier, some guys thought Black Rock Desert would be the perfect location for a weeklong, no-rules party with thirty thousand guests where the main attraction is burning down monumental scale art works. Big stuff, three-story tall house-sized structures, set on fire, late at night, with WWII flame throwers in front of thousands of half drunk or all-the-way stoned, costumed, revelers.

And music. The best electronic music in the world played at the loudest possible volumes that amplification technology could provide.

Burning Man is a little like Mardi Gras only bigger and a lot louder, with huge fire and space ships outlined in brightly colored lights. It is truly an off planet experience; until you need a hospital. Then it's a *real* expensive helicopter ride into Reno a hundred miles to the south. It's twelve miles to the nearest phone, and cell service is non-existent. Pray you never need to be transported off the desert in one of the REMSA ambulances, especially if you are alcohol sick—that can be a very grueling two-and-a-half-hour ride into town that you *will* survive, even if you come to believe it's not possible. Rumor has it they will not sedate you until you arrive at the hospital no matter how insistently you beg or plead.

My daughter graduated from the University of Washington as a nurse after high school and the following summer she'd gone off to Burning Man and married a doctor who had graduated the same year. That winter they moved to Reno to be closer to the annual arts event.

This year, like so many before, she'd arrived a week in advance to work as a volunteer nurse on a late-night medical services shift. Every year, hundreds of dedicated volunteers spend almost a month building and installing the infrastructure that becomes Black Rock City for a week, and every year a few of them get sick or injured in the process, so the medical services outposts are one of the first installations to go up. Once the gates open these outposts become the emergency rooms for the five-mile-wide circular city and serve a steady stream of clients, day and night, with everything from large splinters to heart attacks and diabetic comas. The outposts are well stocked with donated medical supplies and highly qualified volunteer medical professionals who work for little more than a free ticket to the event and access to the event staff food tent.

I was there early to work on one of the large-scale art projects. A team of about twenty of us were building a huge stage surrounded by large, propane-powered fire cannons that would shoot gigantic flames high into the night sky once the event opened to the ticket-holding public. We worked ten-hour shifts in the blazing sun and blistering heat until the wind got so strong we'd have to tie everything down and quit until morning. Effectively we were a well-coordinated group of very brown, very dusty, highly skilled construction workers except that some of us wore tutus, or just bikini bottoms, in the case of the women. Beer drinking and pot smoking was part of the daily routine. We'd been on a very tight schedule for over a week, and now that the stage and fire cannons were complete, it was time for me to prepare to help run the show. That meant riding into town with my girl to get more canned stew and another thirty gallons of water.

"You can tell me anything," I said. Something I'd been telling her, her whole life.

On the day she was born, as she slept on my chest in the hospital, I made a promise to her that no matter what, I would always protect her and listen to her, that right or wrong, win or lose, I would always be right behind her every step of the way.

Over the course of twenty-six years of guiding her into adulthood, I'd come to believe that she did truly love me, and trust me. And while we didn't always agree on everything, I considered her now to be one of my best and closest friends. She said the same about me and acted as though she meant it.

My daughter tightened her lips and nodded as she drove, but she didn't say anything. She clung to the steering wheel as if she were in some kind of death race and stared straight down the road ahead.

"C'mon, darlin', what's up?"

She took a deep breath and said, "We had an incident last night. I haven't slept yet."

"You OK to be driving?"

"I'm fine."

"And that is how I know you aren't fine." I said. Whenever you say you are fine, you are not fine. So what happened?"

She hesitated, and I assumed some third-level medical services department manager with an over-developed sense of self-entitlement had gotten after her for some small lapse in judgment.

"Last night I worked the outpost on the deep playa. Things were real slow—some athlete's foot, a sprained finger, a case of alcohol dehydration was about it—so my backup went home a little after midnight. At about three o'clock, four guys from the temple crew came in carrying an unconscious guy they'd found on the desert and dropped him on a cot. His lips and nose were blue, and he was completely unresponsive. I pinch-tested him and scrubbed my knuckles on his chest to try to wake him up, but I got nothing, not even a blink. His pupils were dilated and unresponsive. I could barely get a pulse on the guy!" Her voice cracked as she continued. "His heart rate was like twelve and he was barely breathing, so I called for a medical assist and started chest compressions to see if I could get a more regular heartbeat. I set my radio down and listened for what seemed like an hour for a response on the radio while I worked on this guy but I heard nothing, so I just kept pumping him and checking for a good rhythm."

Her voice was hoarse and scratchy with unspent tears, and there was residual fear on her face that I'd never seen before. It scared me.

"He was my age, Dad! He had a suicide note on him and a 'Do Not Resuscitate' written on his chest. There I was on my hands and knees, reading his final message to the world, all the reasons he wanted to die, while I'm pumping away on him like he was a crash-test dummy. And all the time singing, *another one comes, and another one goes, and another one bites the dust!*" Her voice broke as she sang the song that had been her CPR rhythm.

She started to cry. "Nobody—fucking nobody! — Would fucking respond to my fucking radio calls!" Her tears turned angry, adult angry, something I hadn't seen in her before.

"I am trying to keep this guy alive with one hand and wake someone up through a radio with the other," she spat, "and I can't get a line in because his veins are all collapsed, and he is going into cerebral posturing, and I'm trying to pump him, and I knew I was going to have to intubate and bag him if I was going to save him, and I am trying to call for help, and the bag is fucking nowhere, and I am alone in the medical tent with the four fucking idiots who brought him in who do nothing but stare at me while I'm frantically trying to save a guy who has just eaten half the drugs on the planet because his girlfriend broke up with him!" she cried. "His girlfriend broke up with him! And he's dying on me, and they can't call for help on a fucking radio?"

She looked directly into my eyes; tears streaming down her face. "I deliver babies, for God's sake, I don't save people's lives!"

She beat the steering wheel with the side of her fist as she drove and cried, "*And another one comes, and another one goes, and another one bites the dust.* Oh, my God!" she cried.

I said nothing. I just let her breathe for a while. It tore my heart out to see her this way, knowing that telling her that everything would be okay would not make it okay. Not this time. She was not fine, and she wouldn't be fine again for a long time to come.

"Oh, my God . . . Oh, my God," she cried over and over again, rocking behind the wheel.

"I know, darlin', "I said softly. "I know." I reached across the seat and caressed her shoulder, trying to take a little piece of her pain and carry it for her so she wouldn't have to carry it alone.

I let a few minutes pass. "Water?" I asked. Offering water to a person in distress was something we'd both learned to do in first responder training before our volunteer shifts on the desert.

She gave me a stricken look and then suddenly laughed. Wiping the tears from her face with her sleeve, she took the frosty-cold bottle I'd pulled from a cooler between my feet. She drank almost all of it and seemed better after a few minutes. She was a strong girl who could handle just about anything. Cool, levelheaded, and professional. She was not what you would expect from a twenty-six-year-old. She carried herself like someone at least ten years older, maybe more. But this had really gotten to her. It got to me, too. I was unprepared for this one, and it rattled me to the core.

"What's cerebral posturing?" I asked two miles closer to Reno.

She wiped her red nose and tear-streaked face with her hands and focused on the long, straight road ahead. I saw her check her rear-view mirror and the speedometer. She didn't answer right away. She waited until she could breathe again. Then, as though reading to me from one of her college textbooks, she began. "Cerebral posturing is when a patient who is experiencing significant brain damage, usually the result of trauma, begins to assume a kind of fetal position. The fists are clenched and turned inward at the chest. The feet point inward toward each other, and the muscles of the face may contort. You see it in severe cases of head trauma or insanity." She paused. "Actually you almost never see it, but when you do, you know that person needs to be in an ICU right now. I studied it in school and heard about it when I worked in the ER in Seattle, but I'd never seen it firsthand— not until last night."

She exhaled hard and leaned back against the headrest. I changed the subject and talked about the installation I was working on and about the theme camp I was with, all members of her extended family of friends from Reno, defined only by a few degrees of separation. I asked her about the people she was camping with and when her husband was going to show up. She told me that he'd arrived the night before but had gone directly to work as medical services director, so she hadn't spoken to him yet.

"No one ever did respond on the radio," she said. "I swear to God, I am going to kick some serious ass for that shit when I get back. That shit is sure as hell going into my report!"

I knew she wouldn't say anything. If she reported that she'd had no backup during an incident, someone would be in violation of the protocols and be in pretty deep trouble. There was supposed to be backup, redundant backup, twenty-four hours a day, no matter what. The instructors stressed that over and over in first responder training. Even I knew that.

"So what finally happened?" I asked.

She lifted her shoulders, as if summoning strength, before continuing her story.

"For some reason, the REMSA paramedics showed up to check in. They were shocked as hell to walk in on that scene when all they wanted was some free coffee. Right away they took over the CPR, thank God, because I was all but done. They zapped him a couple of times and got a better heart rhythm so they packed him for transport. They were able to get a REMSA supervisor out there pronto. He called for the helicopter, and it was there in like a minute. I didn't know what else to do, so I held the IV bag as we rushed him out and loaded him onboard. The helicopter lifted off the second they closed the door, and we watched it fly away. I've never been that close to a helicopter. It was huge! You would have loved all that power. I remember thinking about how much you would have liked to be there when that thing was on the ground."

She went quiet again, and I saw her trying to hold back her tears. Her chin quivered like it had when she was little as she relived the events of the night over and over in her head. She couldn't think about anything else, like the morning after miraculously surviving a horrible accident. She wiped her eyes on the sleeves of her shirt as she drove.

"The guy didn't make it to Reno." She sobbed. "I saw the medics when I was signing out. They said he was dead on arrival."

Tears filled my eyes. "You'll get through this." I said looking away from her.

"I'm not so sure. What if I didn't do everything I should have? What if I missed something? What if I could have done something else? Or what if did something I shouldn't have and a guy died because of me? I'm a labor and delivery nurse, not an ER doctor."

"He was going to die." I said, trying my best to speak with an evenness that masked what I was feeling. "You didn't give him the drugs that killed him.

Maybe you could have performed some kind of miracle from your training, maybe not. Either way, he would have died for certain if you hadn't been there. What matters is that someone who cared whether he lived or died was there with him at the end, and in that final moment, someone cared about him enough . . . loved him enough . . . to try to save his life. You were that someone, and the last thing that guy saw in this world was your beautiful face."

Her expression tightened again. She couldn't speak, so we rode for a time in silence.

I wiped my eyes and leaned my head against the door and thought about the understanding that had come to me on the day she was born. On that day I realized I'd just relinquished my right to die and would have to live as long as humanly possible so that I could be with her at times like this. I had without coercion given up dangerous drugs, very fast motorcycles, and illegal drag racing so I wouldn't hurt myself. And then I took her to Burning Man.

"You need to find some forgiveness?" I asked after a mile or two.

She nodded slowly as she cried.

I paused long enough for what I had to say to gain the momentum needed to help her in some small way.

I leaned in and looked directly at her so there was no mistaking what I was saying. "Then I forgive you." I said.

"Oh, my God!" She began to sob. "That was the worst thing that's ever happened to me."

"I know, baby," I whispered, "and I forgive you, and you need to forgive yourself. You need to look right in here," I said gently tapping her breastbone, "and forgive yourself. You have to believe that under those circumstances you did everything you knew how to do. Right or wrong, good or bad, you did what you had to do, which was more than any other person on the planet did for that guy at that moment.

"You are a gatekeeper, girl. You help people come into this life and sometimes you have to help them go out of it, and you will never know how proud I am of you, because no matter what happened out there, I know in my heart that you did the best you could do, because I know you. I know who you are. I know what you do. And you need to know that in your heart as well."

Tears rolled silently down her cheeks in the unmistakable way they did when she was five years old. Seeing them now broke my heart as surely as they did the day she fell off her bike and skinned her knee.

"I know," I said. "I know."

We drove in silence for a while, snuffing and wiping our faces until we were both breathing normally again.

"Remember, girl," I said, "it isn't about who you are, or what you have, or what God you believe in, or any of that. All that matters in this life is what you do."

We arrived back on the desert with our provisions before noon the next day, and the line at the gate was already a mile long. We had to wait our turn as each car, rental truck, and RV was inspected for stowaways, weapons, or fireworks. Nearly an hour later we were finally waved through when we showed our laminates to the gate staff. She drove us along the long and dusty road leading to the still growing city and out to the Esplanade, the main walking street on Black Rock City's inner perimeter.

"I have to move off site today," I told her, "so drop me at my camp so I can pack."

"Where's your stuff?"

"Right behind the tower." I pointed. "See the tower there?"

Nodding, she pulled up at the gated inner lot beneath a two-story control tower overlooking the stage surrounded by the fire cannons we'd installed. My teammates were a hubbub of activity working on final preparations for the performances that would begin at sundown and continue until morning.

"Did you guys save me a spot at your camp?" I asked her as she slowly steered her way through the throngs of people now out on the desert.

"Yep, we have a nice site for you, right on the corner in front of the port-a-potties. You'll have a hell of a view."

"Nice." I said, stepping out of her car.

"I'll put your water and food box on your campsite," she said.

"Get someone to help you with that water barrel," I said loudly as she backed out. "It's too heavy for you." She smiled at me and gave a short wave, then drove away. I watched as she cut across the playa toward the nine o'clock position of the city before I began loading my gear, bike, tent, tools, and food coolers into the back of my truck. I was backing out of my campsite for the last time when one of the team members hobbled up to my door in a walking cast.

"Hey, darlin'," she said in her mild Texas accent. "You going anywhere near four o' clock?"

Streets and avenues that radiate out from the mile-wide center divide the circular city. The tower project I had worked on was located near Center Camp at six o' clock and Esplanade, the downtown area of the city.

My daughter's camp was at eight thirty and about four streets in. This woman wanted to go to Controlled Burn Camp where most of the people from our team had moved while I was in Reno. Controlled Burn was at four o' clock and Esplanade, almost half a mile in the wrong direction.

She and I had spent a few hours together over the course of the previous week. She'd broken her foot a couple of days before coming to the desert, and I had massaged it very carefully as we sat on an old couch speaking in low tones and watching the sun go down one evening. She'd worn a very short skirt on that blistering hot day. Lying there on that dusty couch, with her foot in my lap, I'd gotten a good look at her vagina.

"Sure!" I said. "Climb in." I picked some good music on my iPod as she worked her way into a comfortable position in the passenger seat. I rolled the truck slowly out of the gated area and onto the open playa toward the other side of the city.

"You've been on the Missing-in-Action list," she said. "Where have you been hiding out? You missed a helluva party last night."

"I went into town with my daughter to re-provision."

"Gerlach?" she asked.

I shook my head. "Reno. We needed food, water and gas for the week, so we went to take showers, eat real food, sleep at her house, then shop for supplies."

"God, I'd love to go to Reno." She sighed. "I haven't had a shower in a week."

"You should go."

"Too far to drive with a stick shift." She pointed at her foot. "I don't have much pain medication left."

We were crossing a promenade that ran between Center Camp and 'The Man', a sixty-foot tall wood statue at the exact center of Black Rock City when I noticed a guy sitting upright on the playa, his legs straight out in front of him, leaning forward from the waist, his hands at his chest, his head down. He was very dusty and not moving.

I pointed out the windshield. "What am I looking at?"

"I don't know." She squinted. "Where?"

"That guy at about two o' clock in front of the truck. What's up with him? We need to give that a look." She spotted him at last and pointed a finger toward the windshield so I wouldn't lose sight of him in the crowd. I pulled up, jumped out of the driver's seat the second the truck stopped moving, ran around the front, and knelt beside him. She eased her way out of the driver's seat and hobbled to where he was sitting.

"Check his vitals," I said.

An EMT and ambulance driver in the real world, she'd already taken his wrist. "He's cold and dry. I can't get a pulse." She frowned. "Go find a radio and get REMSA here now."

My adrenal glands went into overdrive as I searched the crowd for someone with a radio; cops and rangers where usually everywhere, once the gates opened, but I couldn't see any now from my squatting position.

She reached for the man's neck to get a pulse there, and he flopped onto his back. She caught him as he fell and lowered him into the dust. His hands were clenched and remained tight to his chest. His feet, now free to move, turned inward. I could hardly believe what I was seeing.

I stood up and scanned the crowd. Two Black Rock rangers were walking away from us some two hundred yards away.

"Ranger!" I called. They didn't hear me. I ran after them and began screaming, "Ranger! *Ranger*!" One of them turned slowly with a disgusted look on her face. "Call for a medical evaluation right now!" I shouted, my heart racing. "We need REMSA here, now!"

"You don't need to yell at me," she said.

"I am not yelling!" I shouted. "We have a medical emergency, and we need REMSA RIGHT NOW!

She glared at me and shrugged her shoulders. "Dispatch is down, we don't have radio communication."

"Then go help her!" I pointed toward my truck, the limp man, and the woman attempting to help him. The rangers looked at me for a moment before casually moving in that direction. I ran back to the truck ahead of them.

"Their radios are down," I explained loudly to my friend. "See if you can get someone with one that works. I'm going to run!" I pointed toward the circus tent-sized medical facility just beyond the ranger station fifty yards away.

"What?" she shouted over the din of a hundred passing conversations and music.

"I am going to run!" I screamed as loudly as I could, pointing toward the medical tent.

"Yeah, run!" She waved me off. "He's not breathing!"

My heart racing, I sprinted, dodging bicycles and stilt walkers and large groups of people talking and laughing as they strolled, oblivious. Zigzagging through them made the distance to the medical station twice as long. Arriving at last, I threw open the front doors with a bang and surprised a single nurse who was watching a woman vomit into a wastebasket.

"I need REMSA!"

She pointed to the side of the tent. I raced around the corner and found several EMTs talking and drinking coffee around three blue-and-white paramedic ambulances.

"We need a medivac on the Esplanade!"

One of them lowered his cup to look at me. "What have you got?"

Side splitting and panting hard, I crossed the distance to them. "Cerebral posturing!"

The small group began to move, putting down their coffee cups and water bottles. One of them clicked a microphone clipped to his lapel and began to talk into it.

"Where is it?' another of them asked as I ran to the front of the nearest truck.

"There, there!" I looked behind me and pointed back in the direction of my truck. "Follow me! I'm going to run!" I turned toward the Esplanade and jogged in place, but the EMTs were still standing around the truck. "I NEED HELP RIGHT NOW!" I demanded. Finally they crawled into the ambulance.

Ignoring the stabbing pain in my side, I took off and was a quarter of the distance back to the scene when I heard the distinctive braying honk of the ambulance as the vehicle crawled its way across the Esplanade and out onto the open playa. The paramedics in the van caught up with me a few hundred feet before they saw her working on the limp man and gave the siren a few cycles. The crowd looked at the ambulance but didn't really move to let them through.

"He's in cerebral posturing!" I pulled my fists to my chest. The driver turned the siren on and let it run, and the crowd opened a lane for them at last. The driver spotted my truck, and the woman began to wave at him. He accelerated for a moment then came to a stop alongside her. I caught up to them, breathing hard as they unloaded their bags from side bins on the truck and opened the rear doors.

One of the EMTs pulling the gurney out of the ambulance turned to me. "How do you know cerebral posturing? Are you trained? Do you have certifications? Are you medical staff?"

"Completely spent, I bent at the waist and put my hands on my knees. " Not me." I panted hard. My daughter told me."

The gurney hit the ground with a rattle and a thump. "Her?" he asked with a jerk of his head in the woman's direction.

I shook my head. "She's a friend."

"You OK?"

"I'm fine, help her," I said.

She had a look of horror on her face as she stepped away from the guy and allowed the EMTs to take over. After a minute or two I saw the lead guy talking into his radio. He looked up from the microphone on his shirt and said, "We have to clear this area. We're going to evacuate him." He waved his arms indicating a landing spot for the helicopter.

We began to herd the crowd and conscripted the two rangers to help us. I heard the helicopter wind up out near the gate. Not three minutes later it was right over us, blowing up a whiteout dust storm that backed the crowd away pretty quickly.

One of the medics brought a bright yellow backboard from a small door at the back of the ambulance. She and her co-workers rolled the man onto his side and slid the backboard under him then began to strap him down with large Velcro straps. The helicopter was just a few feet off the ground.

One of the medics pointed to a handhold on the side of the backboard and shouted over the scream of the helicopter, "Grab right there! One, two, three!" We lifted in unison. The door to the helicopter slid open, and we loaded him inside, and then backed away.

As the helicopter pilot wound the engine back up, another of the medics asked me, "How did you know it was posturing?"

"My daughter told me about it yesterday. She's a nurse. She had an incident a couple of nights ago, had to medivac a suicide. I don't think he made it."

The medic nodded. "We heard about that one," he said over the 'whup, whup, whup' of the helicopter blades. "Your daughter was on that?"

"Yeah, she was the first responder, and she told me about cerebral posturing."

"Well, this one's probably going to make it. I think we got to him in time. You just saved that man's life," he said, pointing at the ascending helicopter.

I shaded my eyes from the dust and the sun as I watched the helicopter fly over the city and head for the horizon. When I looked around, I noticed a large and growing crowd of spectators who stood watching the helicopter. When it was well away from the city the crowd broke into loud and spontaneous applause.

"I think that truck ran over someone," I heard a voice in the crowd say.

The medics packed their gear and loaded it back on the ambulance. She and I got back into my truck as the crowd began to disperse.

"You OK?" I asked.

"Yeah," she said, "but that guy is fucked up. He was gurgling. I rolled him on his side in case he threw up, but he was barely breathing. Fuck man, how did you see that guy?"

"I don't know, I just saw him. I'm real fucking shaky."

"Yeah, me, too."

I tried to relax for a moment or two before I started the engine, then drove very slowly, not speaking, to her camp on the playa side of the Esplanade. I stopped the truck at last, and she slid out of the passenger seat and came around to my window and kissed me long and passionately on the mouth. "Don't tell," she whispered, then turned and hobbled away.

I sat idling for a while, watching like an outside observer, life at Burning Man going by in front of me. My entire body was quivering as though I had been in very cold water. My legs ached, but my breathing had returned to normal. I eased the gearshift into drive and rolled in the direction of my daughter's camp.

Ten minutes later, I turned the truck into the Black Rock University theme camp and parked near my daughter's small, hand-painted travel trailer with a large portable carport next to it. I slid out of the driver's seat and found I had difficulty walking. My legs were so weak, my body so shaky; I had to be careful not to fall down. I touched each thing I passed to maintain my balance. The hood of a parked car, the tailgate of my daughter's truck, the corner post that held up her tent. She was sitting in a lawn chair, eating a bowl of Japanese soup.

"Hey, Dad," she slurped.

"Hey." I said, trying to sound normal.

She set her soup bowl next to her and gave me a concerned look. "What's up?"

I winced hard and took a long breath as tears sprang to my eyes. "I just saved a guy."

She sat up in her chair. "What happened?"

"I gave one of the girls from Controlled Burn a ride, and I spotted a guy on the playa. We checked him, and he was posturing just like you described."

I had to pause to catch my breath. Her look of concern changed to one of sadness. She got out of her chair and wrapped her arms around my neck.

"We saved him." I said, looking intently into her eyes.

"Oh, my God, Dad," she whispered into my neck.

"I ran and got REMSA, and they told me we saved his life because of what you taught me. You saved that guy's life because you taught me about posturing. That helicopter that just left was the guy."

"That was you?"

"Yeah. The EMTs said we saved his life."

"Oh, Dad!" She broke and began to cry.

I took her into my arms. "I saved someone's life because of what you taught me," I whispered. "We saved him because of you, because of you. Because of what you taught me." We stood holding each other for a time, then sat in the lawn chairs there under the canopy next to her trailer, holding hands.

After a while, she made me some coffee and a package of Japanese soup. I slurped the steaming noodles, thanked her and I told her that I loved her then went back to my campsite.

I stood naked in my tent, rummaging through a large plastic tote that contained my clothes. There, deep down in the bottom, I found what I was looking for. I jerked it out and tossed it onto my dust-covered air mattress.

"Now, where the fuck?" I said as I shuffled through my costumes tote. "Ha! Got it!" I shuffled some more. "There you are, too!"

A few minutes later I emerged. Glorious into the blazing late morning sun. Wearing bright red one-piece long underwear, I tossed a white winter scarf around my neck, pulled a leather aviator's hat onto my head, and finished the look with fur-lined military goggles. Stepping out of my blistering hot tent I slid into my combat boots and marched across the cracked-mud hardpan toward my daughter's trailer.

She saw me coming and laughed out loud, shaking her head. "You look like a comic book superhero!" She called.

"I *am* a comic book superhero." I bellowed in my most heroic voice. "Shall we cruise the playa? I believe adventure awaits!" I said, as I arrived at her side and offered her my elbow.

"Adventure!" she laughed, curling her arm into mine. "Fuck, yeah, man!" she exclaimed.

"Fuck, yeah!" I said.

Made in the USA
Lexington, KY
25 June 2014